Kate Whitsby

Rose's Mail Order Husband

Montana Brides: Book Three

Copyright © 2014 Kate Whitsby
All rights reserved.

ISBN-13: 978-1501053214
ISBN-10: 1501053213

DEDICATION

To YOU, The reader.
Thank you for your support.
Thank you for your emails.
Thank you for your reviews.
Thank you for reading and joining me on this road.

CONTENTS

Chapter 1 1
Chapter 2 5
Chapter 3 9
Chapter 4 15
Chapter 5 19
Chapter 6 23
Chapter 7 27
Chapter 8 31
Chapter 9 35
Chapter 10 41
Chapter 11 45
Chapter 12 49
Chapter 13 53
Chapter 14 57
Chapter 15 61
Chapter 16 65
Chapter 17 69
Chapter 18 75
Chapter 19 79
Chapter 20 83
Chapter 21 87
Chapter 22 91
Chapter 23 95
Chapter 24 99
Chapter 25 105
Chapter 26 111
Chapter 27 117
Chapter 28 123
Chapter 29 126
Chapter 30 131
Chapter 31 137
Chapter 32 142
Connect With Kate 147
Other Books by Kate Whitsby 148
About Kate Whitsby 149
Copyright 150

Chapter 1

Rose only got up in the morning because she was hungry. Oh, and the wedding.

The gnawing in her stomach drove her to get out of bed, get dressed, and go downstairs to breakfast. Her sisters, Violet and Iris, already sat at the table when Rose entered the dining room.

They didn't show any surprise at seeing her, though. They didn't know, or didn't want to know, that she couldn't care less about seeing them.

"You look nice in that dress, Iris," Rose greeted her.

Now, that did surprise them. Their eyes flew open. "Thank you, Rose," Iris replied.

"I don't think I've seen you looking so nice as I have the last couple of days," Rose went on. "Being in love agrees with you."

Iris gasped in surprise, and her eyes welled up with tears. "Thank you, Rose. That means a lot coming from you."

"I guess you changed your mind about marrying Mick McAllister, didn't you?" Rose asked. "I thought you would. You two are made for each other."

Rose took a piece of toast from the plate. The thought of putting it in her mouth and chewing it up made her stomach turn, but she had to eat something now. If she didn't, she would fall over during the wedding ceremony.

No one noticed she hadn't eaten yesterday. They were all too preoccupied with their own troubles. Maybe Jake Hamilton noticed, but her fiancé wasn't around that much. He didn't mention it if he did notice. Would her appetite come back after the wedding? Maybe she wouldn't be able to look at food again.

Rose nibbled the toast and spotted Violet observing her on the sly. That would be just like Violet to notice a person not eating. Rose tried to smile at her, but it came out wrong and turned into a grimace instead. The last thing Rose wanted was her oldest sister hovering over her and worrying about her. She could handle anything else today but that.

"By the way," Violet asked, "what do you want to do about your dress?"

"What about it?" Rose asked.

"It's still in my room," Violet told her. "We haven't laid it out for you yet. Do you want me to bring it to your room?"

"I don't care what you do with it," Rose replied. "Do whatever you want."

"Rose!" Iris exclaimed. "What's the matter with you? You know Violet went to a lot of trouble to make our dresses. You might show a little more appreciation."

"I didn't ask Violet to make the dress," Rose shot back. "I don't even know if I'll wear it."

"Rose!" Iris cried. "How can you be so cruel!"

"What's the matter?" Rose asked.

"Have you changed your mind about marrying Jake?" Violet asked.

Rose cocked her head on one side. "No. What makes you say that?"

"You said you might not wear your wedding dress," Violet repeated. "I thought you might be reconsidering the marriage."

"No, I'll marry him," Rose replied. "I just haven't decided what I'm going to wear. I don't have to wear the dress Violet made. I might wear something else."

Iris gasped again, but Violet kept calm even when Rose saw her wince in pain. "Like what?"

Rose shrugged. "I don't know. I'll have a look through my closet later and decide."

"But you saw the dress Violet made for you," Iris pointed out. "You were happy with it before. What happened to change your mind?"

"You know what happened," Rose replied. "For one thing, I met Jake Hamilton, and that alone changed everything."

"Don't you want Jake seeing you in the dress Violet made?" Iris asked.

"Jake doesn't care what I wear," Rose declared. "I could get married in my bath robe and he wouldn't care."

"How can you be so sure?" Violet asked.

"He told me so," Rose told them. "All he cares about is that we get married."

"Doesn't he care that you wear your wedding dress?" Violet asked. "That seems odd."

"There's nothing odd about it," Rose maintained. "He loves me, and he's not marrying a dress. It's no different from Mick loving Iris in her work clothes."

"Maybe he has some reason for only caring about making the marriage official," Iris suggested. "Maybe he wants to get his share of our fortune before any of us finds out anything about him that could change your mind."

Rose gave an exasperated gasp. "All three of these men want to get their share of our fortune. Jake's no different from Mick and Chuck in that."

"But don't you think…"Iris began.

Rose shoved back her chair. "I should have known better than to come down here when you two were here. I should have known you couldn't keep your suspicions about Jake killing Cornell to yourselves. Now I don't want to talk about this anymore. I'll see you both later when the minister gets here."

She stomped out of the room. She would have liked to eat some more. The bacon on the tray looked good, and it didn't make her queasy the way other food did. Maybe she'd sneak down to the kitchen later and get some.

She just couldn't stand those two meddling in her life. They didn't understand why she wanted to marry Jake—why she *had* to marry him.

She ran back up to her room and shut the door on the world. The ranch world kept turning outside her room, and she even heard the men shouting out by the barn. She would hide in here, away from it all, and come out only in time for the wedding.

She sat down at her dressing table and looked at herself in the mirror, but she'd only just arranged her skirts around the stool when Violet came in.

Chapter 2

Violet laid Rose's wedding dress out on the bed and smoothed the wrinkles out of it. "Here you go, darlin'."

"Thank you," Rose replied without turning around. "I'll have another look at it later when I'm ready to get dressed. Then I'll decide what I'm going to wear."

"Just don't leave the decision until too late," Violet told her. "The minister should be here around eleven, so you'll need to make your decision before then. I can come in later and help you with your hair and tightening your corset, if you want me to."

"Thanks," Rose shot over her shoulder. "I'll let you know."

"I won't mind if you don't wear this dress," Violet went on. "As long as you're happy with how you look, that's all I care about. Don't listen to Iris. You won't hurt my feelings if you decide to wear something else."

"That's good," Rose replied. "You shouldn't be upset, because it's a beautiful dress. You did a wonderful job making it."

Violet stole a glance at her youngest sister's face in the mirror. "What do you see when you stare at yourself like that?

I declare, you do little more than sit there and stare at your own reflection all day long. I don't know what you see in that mirror."

Rose sighed. "I don't know what I see, either. Maybe that's why I have to keep looking, so I can figure it out."

"What is there to figure out?" Violet asked. "You're Rose Kilburn. Who else could you be?"

"I don't know." Rose closed her eyes for a moment, and then she opened them and examined her reflection again. "I don't know who I am anymore. I don't know this small, dark girl. I don't know who Rose Kilburn is, either. The person inside my head is nothing like that girl in the mirror. I've changed so much in the last couple of days that I don't know who I am or what I'm going to be when this wedding is over."

Violet stared at her. "What are you saying?"

Rose shook her head and closed her eyes again. But they wouldn't stay closed. As much as she might want to look at something other than her reflection, she couldn't drag her eyes away from it. "I don't know what I'm saying. I know it doesn't make sense."

"If you don't mind my saying so," Violet remarked, "you don't seem all that happy about this wedding. You don't seem as excited about it as you were before. You know you can tell me if anything happened."

"I appreciate you saying that," Rose replied, "but I don't want to talk about anything. I'm marrying Jake. That's all there is to know."

"You keep saying that," Violet told her. "But you don't seem very happy about it."

"You just don't understand," Rose maintained. "You and Iris assume Jake wants to get the formalities of this marriage out of the way for his own selfish reasons. You don't understand that I have my own reason for wanting the wedding over and done with."

"What is that reason?" Violet asked.

"I want Jake Hamilton bound to me, for better or worse," she told Violet. "I want to hear him take an oath before God that he'll stand by me, no matter what, in life and death, against all obstacles and every kind of trouble."

She glanced over and saw Violet gaping at her in horror. "Something's wrong, isn't it? You're in some kind of trouble, aren't you? Is it Jake? Did he kill Cornell? Has he got something over on you? Is he holding you to some kind of ransom if you don't marry him? Tell me now! If he's threatening you, I'll rip his head off!"

"You don't understand," Rose repeated. "He didn't kill Cornell, and if anybody's holding anybody to ransom, it's me. Now will you please drop it? I don't want to talk about it anymore."

"Okay," Violet agreed. "We won't talk about him anymore. Just tell me what you want to do about the dress. If you want me to take it away, I will. Or I could help you go through your closet and decide what you want to wear. Would you like to do that?"

Rose fixed Violet with such a withering stare that Violet squirmed. "You just won't leave, will you?"

"Can you blame me for wanting to spend the little time we have left with you?" Violet asked. "In a few hours, we'll all be married and busy with our separate lives. We may never get another chance to sit and talk to each other."

"I think we will," Rose replied. "We're not exactly moving away from each other. We'll all still live together at Rocking Horse Ranch. I'm sure we'll get together for meals and celebrations and just to talk. You know how it is when sisters live near each other. Nothing will change between us."

"They already have." Violet put her hand over her mouth and burst into tears. "I don't know what's happening to this family. If I'd known things would go the way they have, I never would have come up with the plan to get these men to come out here to marry us. Our whole family has fallen apart since they came."

Rose studied her sister in the mirror. Then she sighed again, got up from the dressing table, and went to Violet's side. She sat down on the edge of the bed next to the wedding dress and pulled Violet down on her other side. She wrapped her arm around Violet's shoulders and hugged her.

"Don't cry," she told her. "Our family isn't falling apart. We're still sisters, and we'll always be in each other's lives."

"It isn't what I wanted for us at all," Violet sobbed. "I didn't want us all going off in different directions. I feel like you're slipping through my fingers, and I don't know how to hold onto you."

"It wasn't the men coming that did it," Rose told her. "It was Cornell getting killed."

"But Cornell wouldn't have been killed if the men didn't come," Violet cried, "and the men wouldn't have come if I hadn't made the plan for us to marry them. So I'm ultimately responsible for Cornell's death. If I hadn't gotten these men out here, Cornell would still be alive."

"You don't know that," Rose countered. "Cornell couldn't handle us standing up to him, and that was bound to happen sooner or later. When it did, we would butt heads with him, and he would have turned violent. You know this yourself, because you were the first one to experience it. That would have happened whether the men were here or not."

Violet sniffed. "Do you really think so?"

"Of course," Rose replied.

Chapter 3

"I didn't think you believed my story about getting into a fight with Cornell the night he was killed," Violet pointed out. "I thought you doubted me because he never acted violently in the past."

"I guess I changed my mind," Rose muttered.

"What made you change?" Violet asked.

"I don't know," Rose replied. "I didn't really doubt you before. I suppose I just wanted Sheriff Maitland to know Cornell wasn't violent before the night of his death. He was always subtle and calculating. That was his way. But he changed when we started doing things he didn't like and making our own decisions against his wishes. We all changed. We weren't the happy family we were when we were children. Cornell couldn't handle the change."

Violet sniffed. "Do you think we can be a happy family again?"

"Of course we will," Rose insisted. "Cornell's gone, and we're marrying good, kind, strong men who will do the ranch credit and treat us well. We're all going to be happy, just as soon as we marry them."

"Except that one of them is a murderer," Violet reminded

her. "One of them could wind up going to the gallows for killing Cornell, if Sheriff Maitland has his way."

Rose took her arm away from Violet's shoulders and got up off the bed. "No, he won't. No one will hang for killing Cornell."

"You said that last night," Violet recalled. "How can you be so sure?"

"I've never been so sure of anything in my life," Rose declared. "Now let's have a look at my dresses." She opened her closet and rifled through the outfits hanging there.

"I still don't understand why you don't want to wear your wedding dress," Violet remarked.

Rose shrugged. "Call it temporary insanity."

She threw back one dress after another, hardly looking at them before rejecting them. Rose sensed Violet's eyes drilling into the back of her head, and she dared not turn around.

She took her silk opera gown out and held it up. "This one is nice."

Violet said nothing. Rose hung the gown back up and went back to throwing the dresses aside. She took down her white flower print calico dress. "And there's this one. It used to be Mama's, you know, and it's supposed to be worn to other people's weddings."

Violet sighed. "I just don't understand you at all. I don't understand why you want to dress down for your own wedding."

Rose hung up the calico. "Do you know what? I don't understand it, either. I don't understand anything about myself anymore. I only know I'm getting married, and it doesn't matter what I wear. Maybe that's why I don't want to dress up. If I thought it made a difference, I might be more interested in my outfit."

"Doesn't it concern you at all that you're acting so irrationally?" Violet asked. "Aren't you worried you'll lose your footing in the world, acting this way?"

Rose studied her sister. "Not really. I'm not worried about that. As long as I have Jake to ground me, I know I won't lose my footing. I might be acting irrationally now. Maybe I am. Maybe I'm not. It doesn't matter. Once I marry Jake, everything will be okay."

"You're banking an awful lot on this marriage," Violet remarked. "Do you really think that's wise?"

"Whether it's wise or not," Rose maintained, "that's the way it is. Now, come on. Help me with the dress. Which one do you think I ought to wear?"

Violet laughed. "This one, of course!" She pointed to the dress on the bed. "What's wrong with you?"

Rose flung the closet door closed. "Fine. I'll wear it." She stomped back to her dressing table and turned her back on Violet.

Violet recognized the rejection. "I'll go downstairs and talk to Rita about the food. I could come back up here later and help you get dressed if you want."

"If you want to, you can." Rose didn't look at Violet again, and the door shut behind her.

Ah, peace at last. She could let her thoughts drift. If she could only get through the next few hours without further interruption, her life would improve dramatically.

But no, here came Iris. How did they get the idea they could walk in without knocking?

"Do you mind if I talk to you for a while, Rose?" she asked.

"Actually, I do," Rose replied. "I'd rather not talk about anything to anyone right now."

Iris ignored her and sat down on the bed. "We're getting married today, Rose. I think we should talk a few things over."

"Why should we?" Rose asked. "Why should we talk now just because we're getting married?"

"We're sisters," Iris replied. "It's natural for us to talk things over before we get married."

"It might be natural for you," Rose shot back. "It isn't for me."

"Then just sit there and listen so I can talk," Iris snapped. "You might do something for someone else once in a while."

"Did it ever occur to you that I don't want to listen, either?" Rose asked. "What part of sitting in my room with the door shut do you not understand? Are you really so dim that you don't understand I want to be left alone?"

"It isn't normal for you to be alone all the time," Iris insisted, "especially on your wedding day. You've been acting strangely ever since Jake showed up. You've got me and Violet worried sick about you."

"You don't have to worry about me," Rose told her. "I'm fine."

"You shouldn't want to be alone all the time," Iris repeated. "It isn't normal."

"I don't want to see anyone other than Jake," Rose told her, "and I won't see him before the wedding. I don't care if it's normal or not. He's the only one who understands me. What a stupid tradition that is. Now, when I need him the most, I'm not supposed to see him."

"What about me and Violet?" Iris asked. "Are you saying we don't understand you? Are you saying you care more about Jake than you do for us?"

"Do you understand," Rose asked, "that every time one of you—or anyone else, for that matter—bursts in here or tries to talk to me, I have to grit my teeth to get through it?"

"Is it as bad as that?" Iris asked. "Why do you have to grit your teeth? Explain yourself for once. Then I might understand."

"I have to grit my teeth so I don't saying something I might regret later," Rose told her.

"You won't regret talking to people, especially us," Iris maintained. "We're your family."

"Just about everything I say these days, I regret later,"

Rose returned. "If only I could stop talking altogether. That would be a significant improvement on these ridiculous conversations you insist on having with me."

Iris stared at her with her mouth hanging open. "Do you realize just how deeply you've hurt Violet by saying you won't wear her dress?"

"Is that what this is all about?" Rose shot back. "Is that what you came in here to talk to me about?"

"How could you be so heartless to suggest you'd wear anything else?" Iris cried. "You know the trouble she went through to make it for you."

Rose sighed. "Yes, I know."

"So why did you say you wouldn't wear it?" Iris asked

"You obviously haven't talked to Violet," Rose declared. "If you had, she would have told you that I'm going to wear her dress. I don't know why you should care so much what I wear. I could understand why Violet wouldn't want all her hard work to go to waste, but I don't see why you should intrude on my solitude to make her case."

"Maybe I don't like my sister being deliberately hurt for no reason," Iris shot back.

Rose compressed her lips and turned around. "You know, Iris, I've just told you I'm going to wear the dress. Are you happy now? Can you take that and leave? I only have a few hours left before the wedding, and I don't really want to spend them going over what I'm going to wear. It doesn't concern you, so mind your own business."

Iris gasped in exasperation at her and slammed the door on her way out.

Chapter 4

Silence enveloped her at last. But the two confrontations disturbed her so much she couldn't settle back into her usual reverie. She paced around the room for a while, and then snuck out of the house.

She didn't usually like to walk around the ranch. The animals and dust and bugs reminded her too much of the base parts of human nature. She much preferred the airy heights of dreams and fantasies. They could be pure and clean, unlike the sordid muddles of human interactions.

The whole house resonated with the coming anticipation of the wedding. On her way downstairs and through the passage to the back door, she heard Violet and Rita in the kitchen. Rose couldn't decipher whether their voices sounded happy and laughing or arguing bitterly. Rita got mad at Violet more and more frequently, with Violet butting in on everything she tried to do and eventually taking it over to do it herself.

Rose didn't see Iris anywhere.

Outside the back door, her way opened up before her and she knew where she wanted to go. She strode up the path to the top of the hill to the Bird House.

Her guardian and uncle, Cornell Pollard, lived here until just a few days ago. His possessions still littered the whole house. Rose couldn't explain it to herself, but she didn't feel his presence when she went into the house. She felt curiously at home here. When she went there, she saw her future life spread out in all its glorious color.

She meandered through the garden. Nowhere else on the whole ranch attracted her like the Bird House garden. Nowhere else existed purely to please her senses. Watered by an underground spring, its flowers blossomed lush and vibrant in the late spring heat. They nodded to her as she passed, welcoming her.

At the end of the brick walk, she pushed open the door. It squeaked on its hinges, but that, too, sang a friendly note to receive her into the home of her dreams. Her heel rang on the flagstone floor. The breeze rustled the curtains, and the birds sang in the trees overhead. Every sound heralded the coming of the Bird House's new mistress.

Rose ventured into the sitting room and sat down on the couch under the big front window. The leaves of the trees modulated the sunlight, so the light coming into the room blinked in dappled shade. Rose turned her face up into the light and closed her eyes.

She could only escape the relentless examination of her reflection by getting out of her room. If she stayed in the Main House at all, she had no choice but to go back to her room and sit at her dressing table.

What a relief to get away from it! She didn't have to try to solve the mystery of who that strange girl in the mirror was, and she could finally think clearly. She was just getting comfortable when the door swung open again and Jake Hamilton strolled into the house. He caught sight of her and his black eyes glistened.

"Well, well, well," he drawled. "What have we here? Shouldn't you be down at the house getting all dolled up?

Your sisters will be put out if you make yourself scarce at a time like this."

Rose smiled at him. "They're already put out with me, and it isn't because I'm making myself scarce. Quite the opposite."

Jake cocked his head to one side. "How's that? They didn't ask you to make yourself scarce, surely?"

"No, but they might as well have," Rose replied. "They're mad because they say I'm acting strangely."

"And they aren't acting strangely?" Jake countered. "You're all acting strangely, I'd say."

"Do you think so?" Rose asked.

"I'd say so," Jake replied.

"But you've never seen us acting any other way," Rose pointed out. "You never saw us at all before two days ago."

"That's true," Jake admitted, "but I think I can tell when a woman is acting strangely."

"Maybe it's because we're all brides," Rose suggested. "I've heard brides act strangely."

"I don't think so," Jake replied. "I've heard of brides acting strangely, but not this strangely. I think it's because your guardian was just killed. That, and you're marrying against his wishes, so you're doubly confused about everything that's happening."

"I don't feel confused," Rose countered.

"You might not feel confused," he told her, "but you certainly act confused. You act like you don't know your head from your tail."

"That's what Violet and Iris keep telling me," Rose admitted. "If you think so, then maybe there's some truth to it."

"Violet and Iris are acting the same way," he added. "They've got nothing to complain about with you. All three of you are doing it. If they're accusing you of it, it only means they don't recognize it in themselves. I wonder the other guys haven't pointed it out to them."

"Iris certainly has," Rose acknowledged. "Last night, she came into my room and told me she wasn't going to marry Mick. She said he wasn't the man she thought he was, and she said I should reconsider marrying you. Now, this morning, it's all back on. She doesn't know her head from her tail, either."

"I wonder what that was all about," Jake remarked.

"I didn't ask," she replied, "and I don't want to know. I don't want to talk to them at all."

"Oh?" He narrowed his eyes. "Why not? Why don't you want to talk to your own sisters? And on your wedding day, too!"

"You sound like them," she grumbled. "I don't want to talk to anyone. You're the only one who knows what's going on with me anymore, and I wasn't supposed to see you today before the wedding, you know. We're all supposed to be in seclusion."

"I am in seclusion," Jake replied. "That's why I came up here, to be alone. And here you are."

"I came up here for the same reason," she told him.

Chapter 5

"But you're supposed to be getting your dress on and your hair done," Jake reminded her. "The minister will be here soon."

"What about you?" she shot back. "Aren't you supposed to be getting cleaned up and dressed? I don't know what men are supposed to do to get ready for their wedding, but you must be supposed to do something. Maybe the other men should pour tobacco juice on your head or something."

Jake chuckled. "Chuck and Mick are over there in the Fort House polishing every piece of clothing they have. And brushing their suits and all that, too."

"And you aren't?" she asked.

"I already did it once," Jake told her. "I don't need to do it five or six times. I just have to get dressed, comb my hair, and shine my shoes. Then I'll walk down to the Main House and I'll be ready."

"And I'll be there waiting for you," Rose concluded.

Jake smiled. "I should hope so."

"Don't you believe I'll be there?" Rose asked. "Do you doubt me that much?"

"I just know you're acting twitchy, just like the others," Jake told her. "I'm not saying you won't be there. I just won't believe any of this until it actually happens to me. The whole thing seems too surreal. It seems to be happening to someone else, not me."

"I know what you mean," she agreed. "I feel the same way."

He examined her. "You do? I thought you were taking the whole thing in your stride. I thought you were handling it pretty well."

"Someone is," Rose told him. "I don't know if it's me, but someone is. Someone that I don't know or recognize. Someone that I can't control. Someone who wants something different from what I want. I don't know who's handling it all, but somebody is."

Jake raised his eyebrows. "Is it that bad? I didn't think you were that far gone."

Rose looked out the window at the glancing leaves of the trees. The sun glinted off the edges of the leaves, sparkling and dancing. She narrowed her eyes, and the scene swam into a watery haze. She could fade into a sleepy dream in that hazy half-conscious state.

"I'll just be glad when the wedding is over," Rose told him. "I'll be glad when we can come home together and get back to ordinary living. The suspense is killing me."

Jake sauntered around the room, looking at curios on the shelves and pictures on the walls. "I don't know how you can come up here the way you do. I'm lucky I didn't know Cornell Pollard at all. If I did, this place would give me the creeps."

"I don't feel him here at all," Rose replied.

"Don't you?" Jake asked. "He's everywhere you turn up here."

"I don't see him," Rose told him. "Wherever I look, I see our life together, our future, our marriage, our children. I see myself making a home here, the home I never had in the Main House. I see myself giving my children a bath, making meals, mending clothes. I see myself doing all the things Violet does down in the Main House. I see myself living. That's what it is. I've never lived before. But I will live here. I'll live for the first time in my life."

"I suppose that's a good thing," Jake remarked.

"I can't wait," she replied.

Jake walked over to the kitchen and looked out the window at a neighboring hill with a cluster of cypress trees on its peak. "And there's his grave right over there. We'll always be able to look out and see it, and he'll be able to watch over us, too."

"He won't watch over us," Rose retorted. "He's dead."

"So what do you propose to do with all his personal possessions?" Jake asked. "Are you just going to leave the place furnished the way it is now, and work around his things?"

"Of course not," she shot back.

"What are you going to do with them?" he asked again.

"Get rid of them, of course," she snapped. "I don't want his things in my house. If the others want any of it, they can have it. Otherwise, we'll just dump the whole kit and caboodle."

"You can't be serious!" Jake exclaimed. "There's some very valuable stuff here."

Rose looked around. "If there is, we'll keep it. I don't have any reason to get rid of or keep anything in particular. I don't feel anything for his things one way or the other."

Jake shook his head. "No wonder your sisters think you're acting strangely. At least Violet is crying for Cornell every once in a while. It isn't natural for you to feel nothing at all for him. He was your uncle and your guardian for most of your life, after all."

"He's a lump of rotten flesh now," she spat. "Let him rot over there on the hill. I don't care, and I don't see him watching over me when I look out the kitchen window. He's gone, and good riddance."

"That's easy for you to say," Jake countered. "You don't have that Sheriff breathing down your neck."

"Is he breathing down your neck?" Rose asked. "I didn't know he questioned you after that meeting in the parlor, unless there's something you haven't told me."

"He doesn't have to question me," Jake replied. "He's hunting around the place. Maybe he's here right now. I don't know, but it's only a matter of time before he finds out the truth about Cornell's death."

"I don't care." Rose stared out the window at the leaves.

"Maybe you don't, but I do," Jake told her.

"Why should you care more than I do?" she shot back. "You don't have anything to worry about from that Sheriff."

"You don't think so," he replied, "but I do. You don't see it, but I do. I've seen it before. The Sheriff will follow his nose, and it will lead him to me."

"Don't worry," Rose insisted. "We'll be married in a few hours, and nothing can come between us after that."

Chapter 6

Jake sidled over to the couch and sat down. "I'm glad you still want to marry me."

"Why wouldn't I?" Rose asked.

"After everything that's happened," Jake replied, "you might reconsider. You might decide it was all too much. You might think your sisters are right, that I'm not the man you thought I was. Who knows? You could come up with any excuse in the book."

"You *are* the man I thought you were," Rose told him. "Aren't we sitting here together, in our future home, making plans for the future? How could that be happening if you weren't the man I thought you were?"

"I just thought you might think I was trouble," Jake explained. "I don't know. I wondered if you would want to go through with it, after Cornell died and the Sheriff started in on us."

"I want to go through with it," Rose told him. "I want to go the whole hog. I want the cow, the milk, and the whole dairy farm. You should know that by now. We've been through enough together already. We should stick it out to the end."

"I just hope we don't wind up in over our heads," he replied.

"Why would we?" she asked.

"You never know what's gonna happen," Jake told her. "Things could go squirrely when you least expect it."

"They won't," she insisted. "I'll make sure of it."

"You?" he repeated. "You'll make sure of it? Very reassuring. Big help, that is."

"Come on," she shot back. "Stop raining on my parade. I'm getting married, and you're going to make me upset if you keep talking like that. Forget about the Sheriff. He can't touch us."

Jake let his hand drop onto hers where it rested on the seat of the couch. "If I stop thinking about the Sheriff, I start thinking about….other things. Things I really shouldn't think about."

"You always were a bad sort," Rose returned. "You can't keep your mind on the job."

Jake slid over next to her. His hand closed around her fingers, and he picked up her hand in both of his. "You know what? We're coming home to this house after the wedding. Where are we going to sleep—in his bed?"

"I changed the sheets and blankets," she assured him.

"When did you do that?" he asked.

"Yesterday," she told him. "I came up when you were out on the range with Chuck and Mick. I found some clean sheets and blankets in that trunk by the bed, and I changed everything. I took the old ones down to Rita."

"Aren't you at all worried about your sisters finding out?" Jake asked. "They get upset if we even glance in the direction of the Bird House."

"I didn't tell Rita where the sheets came from," Rose told him, "but I think she knew anyway. She's a lot sharper than she lets on. She'll find a way to cover for us when Violet comes poking around."

"You've got the whole thing worked out, haven't you?" he asked.

"I told you," Rose exclaimed, "I want this. I want to be married to you, and I want to come home to this house after the wedding, and I want us to be comfortable here. I want to get my life started before another sun sets on this place. I think we've earned it."

He pulled on her arm and drew her towards him. "We have earned it." He kissed the back of her hand.

Rose closed her eyes and melted into the velvety touch of his lips on her skin. She could bathe all her wounds and hurts with that soothing balm. Did he even know how precious his kiss was to her? Did he suspect? He didn't welcome declarations of undying love, but he seemed to know, almost better than she knew herself, what lurked in her heart. When he looked at her, he saw the truth written in her soul.

With her eyes still closed, she felt the soft whiskers of his moustache brushing the back of her hand. The breath from his nostrils tickled the tiny hairs on her fingers. A shudder ran up her spine.

With an immense effort, she tore her eyes open, only to find them locked in Jake's penetrating stare. His eyes laughed and drilled into her core all at the same time. Rose struggled to breathe.

He traced the outline of her cheek and jaw with his fingertips, and a warm, syrupy sensation rippled down in the bottom of her stomach. She held herself perfectly still, bearing the throbbing of her pulse through her flesh. If she moved at all, he might mistake her movement for resistance.

He kissed the back of her hand again, and his hands rubbed up around her wrist and further along toward her elbow. Then his arm slid around her back, and she sucked in her breath as he leaned her back against the couch.

He gazed down into her eyes, and his face loomed closer. Her lips quivered in anticipation, but he didn't drop down to her. He hung there, and then his head fell onto her breast.

Her body lay in his embrace, panting, yearning, reaching for more, but he didn't go any further. He rested his cheek against the bodice of her dress, and her heartbeat made the hair on the back of his neck dance with each pulsation.

She waited until she knew he wouldn't move any closer. Then she covered that slender neck with her hand and massaged it. The curls at the ends of his hair rolled up under her fingers. She touched the delicate hairs going down each side of his spine, and examined the pores of his skin.

Her heart slowed down, and the burning quicksilver in her guts cooled, but still her body clung to him for its very life.

"Your sisters would have me strung up if they saw us like this," Jake murmured into her chest.

"Don't you believe it," Rose replied. "What do you think Mick and Iris were doing in the barn when Cornell was shot?"

"And don't forget Chuck and Violet," Jake reminded her. "They said they were talking in the Fort House just before it happened."

"They were probably doing a lot more than we are now," Rose continued. "Anyway, we're as good as married. Then no one will have anything to say about anything anybody else does."

Chapter 7

"The minister will be here soon," he remarked. "You should get up to your room before he comes."

He sat up, but she stayed reclined on the couch, looking up at him. She didn't answer him. She finally looked away toward the window.

"What's bothering you?" he asked.

"The dress," she told him. "The dress Violet made for me."

"What about it?" he asked.

"They got mad because I said I didn't want to wear it," she told him.

"Why don't you want to wear it?" he asked.

"The sleeves are ruffled," she told him. "The sleeves end here, just below the elbow, and then there's a ruffle that goes down the rest of the way. When you lift your arm, your forearm is visible."

"Oh, I see," he replied. "So what are you going to do about it?"

"They made such a stink that I agreed to wear it," Rose told him. "I didn't want to, but Violet went to a lot of trouble to make our dresses, and both of them got very offended when

I said I'd wear something else. So I guess I have to wear it. It could cause a problem."

"I see," he replied. "Well, we'll just have to deal with it when the time comes."

"With any luck," she continued, "the Sheriff will stay away until after the service. He said he would try to. That will give me a chance to change back into a dress with regular sleeves."

Jake snorted. "I think that was his polite way of saying he's coming. Besides, if what you say about the dress is true, you could still have some explaining to do to your sisters and Chuck and Mick. It could get sticky."

"So I'll explain," he replied. "What could be simpler?"

"I don't know why you didn't just explain in the first place," Jake remarked. "Then we wouldn't have to sneak around like this."

Rose shrugged. "Humor me."

"I am," he replied.

Rose sat up. "I guess we should go back down. There's no point pawing through every detail of the situation right now. Let's get the wedding out of the way. Everything will be much clearer afterwards."

"So you keep saying." Jake strolled through the room, studying the objects and furniture again. "Doesn't it bother you in the least that this is his house?"

"Not in the least," Rose declared. "He deserved to die, and he deserved to die in a much more painful, tortured, excruciating way to pay for what he did."

Jake shook his head. "You're a hard one, you are. I didn't know you were so hard."

"What's the matter?" Rose shot back. "You told Violet yourself that the only thing to do with a man like Cornell was to shoot him like a mad dog. He should be grateful he died as quickly and painlessly as he did. There are worse ways a man can die."

"Just don't tell your sisters that," Jake told her. "They'll go into hysterics if they hear you talking that way. Come to think of it, don't tell the Sheriff, either."

"I will tell them," she declared. "I'll tell anyone who asks."

He meandered toward the door. "Are you coming? I'll walk you out."

"I'm coming," she replied.

He met her at the door and took her hand. They went out into the garden, and Jake shut the door behind them. "I like this part of the house best of all. I don't have to see him here."

"In a little while," Rose told him, "you won't see him inside, either. We'll get rid of his things, and we'll rearrange the house, and we'll make it our own. Then you'll forget all about him."

"I don't think I'll ever forget him," Jake replied.

They walked a little further to the edge of the garden. A hedge of juniper blocked any view in or out. Jake pulled Rose close to him again. This time, his lips sailed in toward her and landed on her mouth. "It sure is nice here."

"I love it," Rose replied. "I always loved the Bird House. I hated Cornell for living here, because I couldn't come here when I wanted to without running into him. I used to come and hide in the garden when I knew he was working in the Main House library. This was my secret hiding place, and neither he nor my sisters ever knew. I could run away when I heard him coming."

"What would he have done if he knew?" Jake asked.

"He probably would have forbidden me to come here at all," she replied. "He didn't want anyone coming here. It was his sanctuary."

"I can understand why," Jake told her. "These hedges keep you completely hidden from the rest of the ranch. You can forget all about the rest of the world and disappear into your own little inner world."

"That's what I like about it," Rose agreed.

He kissed her again. He pulled back and gave her a shy smile. "I'll guess I'll see you in a little while." He put his head to one side. "It seems like a long time. I don't know why."

"The sooner, the better," she agreed.

They shared another lingering kiss, and a knowing look, and then they slipped out through the opening in the hedge.

Chapter 8

Rose ran down the hill to the Main House. Just inside the back door, she turned to rush up the stairs, but she stopped when she heard Violet and Iris talking in the kitchen.

"I'm telling you, Violet," Iris was saying, "she's hiding something. The only explanation is that she and Jake planned to kill Cornell, and now she's worried about getting caught."

"She doesn't seem at all concerned to me about getting caught," Violet returned. "Every time we question her about it, she seems quite certain neither she nor Jake will be held responsible for the murder. She might know something, but maybe she knows who did it and she knows it wasn't her or Jake."

"But that would mean that either Mick or Jake did it," Iris reasoned, "and we know they didn't. No, it has to be them. Maybe she planned the whole thing with him in her letters to him. Maybe she got herself a mail-order husband who would help her get rid of her guardian, and now they've carried out her plan."

"How can you think such a thing about your own sister?" Violet cried.

"What else is there to think?" Iris shot back. "Have you

got another explanation for the way she's acting? It just doesn't make any sense."

"I certainly don't understand it," Violet replied. "I've never seen her like this."

"And can you believe that business about her not wearing the dress you made for her?" Iris exclaimed. "I've never heard anything so outrageous in all my life. She's always been such a meek little lamb. If he didn't influence her to kill Cornell for the house, then the only other possibility is that she influenced him."

"She can't be a murderer," Violet wailed. "She just can't be! She's our sister."

"I'm sure most murderers are somebody's brother or sister or son or daughter," Iris remarked. "They must be related to somebody. We're no different from everybody else. You have to admit that Rose has always been a little queer. Maybe she went off the deep end. Who knows what drives a person to kill another? And for such a paltry prize as a house! It doesn't bear thinking about!"

Violet sobbed, and Rose imagined her covering her mouth with her hand the way she did when she got distressed. Dear old Violet! She would defend Rose until the end of the world.

Iris was another story altogether. A groundswell of hatred for her middle sister rose up in Rose's heart, but she couldn't face them both again. She'd held out against almost nonstop assaults from both of them ever since Cornell died.

She turned away toward the stairs and took a couple of steps when her two sisters breezed out of the kitchen and nearly collided with her at the door.

"Oh!" Iris exclaimed. "I didn't know you were here, Rose." She bit off the end of her words.

"Of course you didn't know I was here," Rose returned. "If you had known, you wouldn't have been talking about me where I could overhear your conversation."

"Did you hear....?" Violet began.

"I heard every word," Rose told them.

"Oh, I'm sorry!" The tears Violet she just dried started running out of her eyes again.

"You don't have to apologize," Rose assured her. "I already knew what you both think. You've told me to my face you think Jake is a murderer, and that I'm either protecting him or guilty myself. What is there to apologize for? You can think whatever you want."

"You've never denied it," Iris pointed out.

"I've told you before that Jake is not a murderer," Rose maintained. "But I can see there's nothing I can say to convince you."

"Why don't you just tell us what it is you know?" Iris suggested. "If we understood your thinking, we might believe you were innocent."

"No, I won't tell you anything," Rose snapped. "If you can't believe I'm innocent, I'm not going to make it easier for you."

"Then we have no choice but to think you're guilty," Iris concluded, "or that Jake is guilty and you're protecting him."

Rose took hold of the banister. "I really don't care what you think. I'm very happy to have you think me a murderer. At least we all know what we think of each other. That clears the air."

Violet laid her hand on top of Iris's on the banister. "Don't walk away, Rose. Don't leave with this ugliness hanging over us. Let's work this out so we all understand each other. Let us know what's going on with you. Don't let us think the worst of you."

"I know you wouldn't think the worst of me, Violet," Rose replied. "I know you would think the best of me no matter what happened. But if Iris wants to believe I'm protecting Jake from a murderer charge, that's okay with me. I'll admit that all the evidence points to him. I can't deny that. But you'll just have to believe me. I know more about him than you do, and he's not a murderer."

"I just can't believe you," Iris told her. "You've been acting so strangely, and you've said some very cruel and nasty things to Violet and me. It's easier for me believe you're involved in this somehow. You've given me no choice."

"That's all right." Rose replied. "I don't mind."

A rap at the front door interrupted them, and Violet answered it. She held the door aside, and Sheriff Tom Maitland strutted into the hall.

"Mornin', ladies," the sheriff greeted them. "Nice day for a wedding, don't you think?"

Chapter 9

"Good morning, Sheriff," Violet replied. "I trust your investigation is progressing well."

"Oh, it is," he assured her. "As a matter of fact, that's why I'm here. I'm here to arrest Jake Hamilton for the murder of Cornell Pollard."

The sheriff and Violet and Iris spun around when they heard a sudden cry from Rose. "But you can't arrest Jake!"

"Oh, but I can," Sheriff Maitland replied. "I can, and I will."

"You can't!" Rose cried again. "He didn't do it."

The sheriff examined her with a jaundiced eye. "You'll have to forgive me, young lady, if I don't take the word of a woman who's waiting for him at the threshold of the altar as an iron-clad profession of his innocence. You see, there's a preponderance of evidence that points to him as the most likely suspect."

"Would you mind telling us what that evidence is?" Violet asked. "Not that I doubt your investigative abilities, you understand, Sheriff. It's just that, as you say, Rose is about to marry Jake, and if you're going to arrest him, it would help if we heard what evidence you're citing as proof of his guilt."

"I didn't say I had proof of his guilt," Sheriff Maitland corrected her. "I only said I had a preponderance of evidence, and that's all I need to make an arrest. The court will have to establish proof of guilt. But since you ask, I'll tell you what the evidence is."

"I appreciate it," Violet replied.

"I think I can eliminate you three ladies as suspects," the sheriff told her. "And I believe that fella McAllister has an alibi for the time of the murder, even if it is his own sweetheart that's giving him one. And I don't believe Mr. Ahern could have gotten all the way around the other side of the house and back up to the Fort House in time to meet Miss Violet at the corner of the fence. So that eliminates him."

"But just because Jake doesn't have an alibi doesn't make him guilty," Rose pointed out.

"No, but there is other evidence," Sheriff Maitland replied. "As I told you all in the library yesterday, one of the slugs that hit Cornell in the chest lodged in his ribs. It didn't penetrate his chest. I could see the end of it sticking out."

"Yes, I remember," Violet replied. "That's how you knew the gun that killed him was 38 caliber."

"That's right," the sheriff confirmed. "Jake Hamilton is the only one of the three men who carries 38 caliber side arms. The slug lodged in Cornell's chest had some unique markings on it. I think if I found the gun that fired the slug, I could match it to the slug by some features of the firing chamber in the gun. See what I mean?"

"You could also use the same evidence to clear Jake of any wrong-doing," Violet suggested. "You could see that his gun didn't kill Cornell."

"I could," Sheriff Maitland agreed, "but to do that, I would have to examine the gun, and I won't be able to do that until I lay my hands on Mr. Hamilton. And I couldn't very well tip him off that I was lookin' for him without placing him under arrest. He might run off in the meantime. Anyway, I'm here to arrest him, and I'll examine the gun afterwards. You don't happen to know where I can find him, do you?"

"As far as I know," Violet replied, "he's up in the Fort House with the other men. He should be getting ready for the wedding."

"He should be," Sheriff Maitland returned, "but he isn't. I just went up to the Fort House to look for him there, and there's no one there. That's why I came down here."

All three women gasped in astonishment. "No one there? Where are they?"

"That's what I want to know," Sheriff Maitland replied.

"But they should be up there getting ready for the wedding," Violet cried. "What can have gone wrong, if they aren't there?"

"We have to find Jake Hamilton," the Sheriff declared. "He's under arrest for murder." He turned to Rose. "You don't know where he is, do you, young lady?"

Rose stared at him, then at her sisters. "I don't know where he is."

"Where was the last place you saw him?" the Sheriff asked.

Rose staring in distracted confusion from one face to another.

"If you know where he is, Rose," Iris put in, "you should tell the Sheriff now. You don't want to be held responsible for protecting an accused killer."

"I really don't know where he is," Rose wailed. "I just left him up at the Bird House."

Iris scoffed in scorn, but Rose interrupted her.

"I didn't intend to meet him there," she insisted. "You have to believe me. I just went out for a walk, and I wound up in the garden up there. Then I went sat on the window seat inside." She turned back to the Sheriff. "I'm going to live there after the wedding, you understand. I was just thinking about what it's going to be like. I didn't know he would show up there, too."

"But he did show up," Sheriff Maitland prompted.

"We were just talking there," Rose told him. "Then we left. I came back here, and he went back to the Fort House. We agreed we would meet again in front of the minister. We were both going to get dressed for the wedding. That's the last time I saw him. I swear it!"

"I sure hope you're telling me the truth," Sheriff Maitland growled, "because if I find out you're protecting him, I could charge you with accessory to the murder. You're already under suspicion of planning it in advance to get Cornell's house."

"We didn't plan it in advance!" Rose shrieked. "Everyone keeps saying that, but we didn't. I could show you all the letters we exchanged in arranging our marriage to prove it to you."

Sheriff Maitland nodded. "You might want to hold onto those as evidence."

She opened her mouth, but only an inarticulate squeak came out. She wrung her fingers together, and she would have run for her life if she could have moved her legs at all.

"If he isn't in the Fort House," Violet put in, "then where is he?"

"And where are Chuck and Mick?" Iris added. "If they aren't getting ready for the wedding, where are they? The minister will be here soon, and they won't be ready."

"Neither will we, if this keeps up," Violet pointed out.

The front door opened behind the sheriff, and Chuck Ahern and Mick McAllister entered the house. Their eyes widened when they spotted the sheriff.

"Mornin', Sheriff," Chuck began. "What can we do for you this mornin'?"

"As I was just explaining to the ladies here," Sheriff Maitland replied, "I'm here to place Jake Hamilton under arrest for the murder of Cornell Pollard. You wouldn't happen to know where he is, would you? You or Mr. McAllister here?"

"I don't know where he is," Mick replied, "but he just rode off. He just got his horse out of the barn and rode away, not five minutes ago."

Chapter 10

Sheriff Maitland whirled around. "What?"

"He's gone," Mick repeated. "He just left."

"Which way did he go?" the Sheriff bellowed.

Mick jerked his thumb across the range toward the west. "Up the canyon. I don't know where he was going, but he was galloping pretty hard by the time he cleared the fence. I thought at the time he was headed up to the range to check on something about our herd. I didn't think much of it. I just thought he wanted to get out for a ride before the wedding."

A sob broke out of Rose's mouth. "He can't be! He can't have run off, not when we're about to get married!"

No one listened to her.

"You men," Sheriff Maitland waved his hand to include Chuck and Mick, "I'm deputizing you two to come with me and bring him back. He can't have gone far in a just a few minutes, and you two know the area better than I do."

Chuck and Mick glanced at each other. "We don't know the land at all," Mick told him. "We both got here two days ago. If you want someone who knows the land, you should talk to Iris."

"I'm not deputizing a woman," the Sheriff snarled. "I'm taking you both. Now, let's go."

"But we're supposed to be getting married in less than two hours," Violet cried. "You can't take them now!"

"Oh, yes, I can," Sheriff Maitland shot back. "This is a matter of public safety. We can't let an accused murderer run free. We've got to bring him in, and if you don't come, I'll arrest the whole pack of you for obstruction of justice. Now, turn around and get your horses out and let's go."

He herded Chuck and Mick out of the house over the protests of the women.

The door slammed on them, and the three sisters faced each other again. Rose's breath came out in gasps, and her eyes darted every which way, searching for help from somewhere. "This can't be happening! This can't be happening! Not now!"

Iris and Violet blinked at her. "Well," Iris remarked. "I guess that's it."

"'It'?" Rose shrieked "How can you say that's it?"

"You heard him," Iris replied. "He just deputized Chuck and Mick. They'll track down Jake and arrest him for Cornell's murder. Then our lives will go on."

"He can't arrest Jake," Rose maintained. "Not now! We're about to get married."

"You can't marry Jake," Iris told her. "He's a wanted murderer."

Rose covered her ears with her hands, clamped her eyes shut, and screeched at the top of her lungs. "He is not a murderer!"

"You keep saying that," Iris replied. "But what are you going to do about it? You can't stop the sheriff from arresting him."

"I can stop him," Rose maintained.

"You?" Iris shot back. "You can stop him? How?"

Rose looked toward the door. "I can tell him Jake didn't kill Cornell."

"Do you really think he'll believe you?" Jake asked. "He has no reason to believe you. You're his fiancé."

"You heard him say," Rose pointed out, "he believes your story about being alone with Mick in the barn. You have no one to verify your story, but he believes you."

"Of course he believes us," Iris replied. "One of us isn't the owner of the murder weapon. Besides, you'll say and do anything to protect Jake. Someone had to kill Cornell. If you can't tell the sheriff who really did it, then protesting Jake's innocence doesn't mean a thing."

"This can't be happening," Rose wailed.

"It is happening," Iris told her. "He killed Cornell, and now he's going to pay the price. You should be glad they're taking him in before you married him. Then you wouldn't be married to a murderer. Anyway, he ran off and left you. He couldn't marry you now, even if he wanted to."

"Iris is right," Violet put in. "It's better for you to stay single than to marry a wanted man. You can always get another mail-order husband who isn't mixed up with the law."

"How can you say that?" Rose gasped. "You know I don't want anything else in the world than to marry Jake."

Violet patted her on the shoulder, and the tears streaked down her cheeks. "I know you don't, but it's better this way. He'll either be on the run, or in jail for this murder. He won't be with you. It's better for you not to marry him. Then no one can tie you to him. You're free to marry someone else."

"I'll never marry anyone else," Rose sobbed. "No one can ever take his place in my life. I'll be alone for the rest of my life if I can't have him."

"You say that now," Iris replied. "After a while of him being gone, you might feel differently. Besides, we'll need another man to run the ranch. Now that Jake's gone, we're a man short."

Rose shook her head. "No. That won't happen. Jake will clear his name, and then he'll come back, and then we'll get married. I'll tell the Sheriff he didn't kill Cornell, and then he'll leave, and Jake will come back. That's what I'll do."

"How will Jake clear his name?" Iris asked. "Not only is he in possession of the murder weapon, he *owns* the murder weapon, which means it wasn't likely to be out of his possession at the time of the murder. And going on the run to avoid arrest only makes him look even more guilty."

"But he didn't kill Cornell," Rose insisted. "You have to believe me."

. "You already know how I feel about Jake," Iris told her, "but you have to be realistic about this. It's virtually impossible that he could ever convince anybody that he's innocent, with evidence like that against him."

Rose collapsed into another flood of weeping. "I know it. I was so convinced I could stop him from taking responsibility for it."

"But he *is* responsible for it," Iris pointed out. "Why should you stop him being held responsible? If he killed Cornell, he should pay the price for it."

"You don't understand," Rose cried.

"Explain it to me, then," Iris shot back. "Explain to me what makes you so convinced he didn't do it. Explain to me how he could have been in possession of the murder weapon at the time of Cornell's death without being responsible for killing him. I would love to hear you explain that."

Rose stared at Iris with tears streaming down her cheeks. She opened her mouth, but broke down in sobs again. "I can't. I want to, but I can't."

Violet intervened. "Leave her alone, Iris."

"I'm trying to help her," Iris argued.

"This isn't helping," Violet shot back. "Can't you see her heart is breaking? Leave her alone."

"I know her heart is breaking," Iris replied. "But you have to admit, this could be the best thing to happen to her."

Chapter 11

Rose started to say something else, but just as quickly, she swallowed her tears and squared her shoulders. This couldn't be happening. Something would happen to stop the Sheriff from arresting Jake, to stop him from running away to avoid arrest.

He couldn't leave! He couldn't! Not after all the hope she invested in marrying him. She never cared about anyone the way she cared about Jake, and now, when he held the key to her heart, he was gone!

Curse that Sheriff, and curse Cornell for dying, and curse everybody in the world! If she couldn't marry Jake, what was the point of anything? What was the point of living at all, if she couldn't marry the only man in the world worth marrying?

The dam holding her emotions back broke apart, letting them rush out into the open. "It doesn't matter now. You both finally got what you wanted. The sheriff has gone to get him, and when he comes back, he'll take Jake away, and I won't be able to marry him. You can both be happy now. You got what you wanted."

"This isn't what I wanted," Iris replied. "I mean, I didn't want you to marry him. But I wanted you to decide that for yourself. I didn't want you to be abandoned at the altar, and I didn't want it to happen so suddenly, within hours of your wedding. It isn't fair to you. The Sheriff should have a heart."

Rose tried to think of something tough and cutting to say, but she burst into tears instead. She covered her eyes with her hand, and her sobs forced themselves out of her body with such force she feared they would split her in half.

Iris and Violet laid their hands on her to comfort her, but she only cried all the harder, and they wrapped their arms around her to protect her from her pain.

"I don't know what I'm going to do," she sobbed. "I don't know what I'm going to do now that he isn't going to marry me. I thought everything would be all right once we were married, that marrying him would take care of everything else. I've banked all my hopes on him, and now he's gone. I know he only ran off because he doesn't want to get arrested. I can't blame him for that. This is all my fault."

"How is it your fault?" Iris asked. "The sheriff can match the bullet he took out of Cornell's chest with Jake's gun. I always thought he was guilty. Now we have the proof."

A loud sob tore out of Rose's throat, and Violet turned on her middle sister. "That's not helping anything right now, Iris. If you can't find a way to help Rose, then keep it to yourself."

Iris pulled her head down between her shoulders. "I'm sorry. I shouldn't have said that. Rose, listen to me. Whether he's guilty or not, it's better for you if you stay unmarried."

With a loud cry, Rose tore herself away and fled up the stairs to her room. She slammed the door and threw herself down on her face on her bed. She buried her face in the pillow and gave vent to her grief.

Not like this. Not like this, kept repeating in her brain. Why did it have to be like this? Why couldn't all this horror wait until after they were safely married? Then she could rest, secure in the knowledge that his heart protected and sheltered hers from whatever demons haunted her. No one could touch either of them once they were married.

She kept her face covered until the greater part of her upheaval passed. Even then, she didn't get up. What was the point of facing the world without him in it? She would lie on her bed forever. She would petrify there, and no one would ever know the truth about her and Jake Hamilton.

Her tears dried on the burning iron of her cheeks. The swollen torture of her eyelids and lips gave testimony to her grief and disfigured her previous anticipation for her wedding.

The sound of men shouting and horses neighing drew her back to the world. She peeked out from behind her curtains and saw a rider pulling his mount up to the barn yard fence. Pete Kershaw met him there and took hold of his horse's bridle.

Rose pulled her head into the room and heard her sisters' voices outside on the landing. She opened her door and met them there.

"The minister's here," Violet told them. "What are we going to do?"

"There's nothing we can do," Iris answered. "We haven't got any men to marry. We'll have to call off the wedding."

"Should we send him home to Butte?" Violet asked. "Or should we try to keep him around, just in case the men come back?"

"How can we keep him around?" Iris replied. "We have no idea when the men will get back. They could be gone for weeks."

"Do you really think so?" Violet asked. "Don't you think they'll be back by tonight?"

"Tonight?" Iris repeated. "Not a chance!"

"Why not?" Violet asked. "Jake can't be too far ahead of them. Once they find him, they'll come back here."

"What do you think they'll do, once they find him?" Rose asked between hiccups of sobs.

Violet took her hand. "The Sheriff will almost certainly

take him back to Butte to stand trial for Cornell's murder." She turned back to Iris. "But that still doesn't solve the problem of what to do about the minister. Should we send him away?"

"I don't see the point of keeping him around," Iris told her.

"But just think about it," Violet replied. "Imagine if we send him away, and then the men come back tonight, and we have to send for the minister to come out and marry us all over again. Wouldn't it make more sense to keep him here? Maybe we can get him to marry us tonight or tomorrow morning."

Iris shrugged. "I guess that's a possibility. But where are we going to put him?"

"There's always the Bird House," Violet suggested. "No one's staying there." She stole a glance at Rose. "Rose and Jake won't be staying there tonight."

"They won't be staying there at all," Iris shot back. "The Sheriff won't bring Jake back here—not to stay, anyway."

Rose choked on a sob.

"All right," Violet agreed. "We'll ask him to stay on, just for a day or two, and try to marry us when the men come back. We'll offer him the Bird House in the meantime."

"We just won't tell him the previous occupant was murdered here two days ago," Iris added.

"And we'll have to change the sheets," Violet pointed out.

Chapter 12

"I already did that," Rose told them.

Both of her sisters rounded on her. "You what?"

"I changed the sheets on the bed," Rose repeated.

"When did you do that?" Violet cried.

"Yesterday," Rose told her. "After the sheriff finished talking to us about Cornell's death, Jake and the others went up to the range. I did it then."

Violet pressed her lips together and turned away, but Iris narrowed her eyes at Rose. "That was a little bit presumptuous of you, don't you think?"

"Why?" Rose asked. "Cornell was dead, and I told you I wanted to live in the Bird House, so it only made sense to assume Jake and I would go live there after the wedding. Why? What's the problem."

"Cornell's body was hardly cold," Iris pointed out, "and already you're planning to move into his house."

"What are you trying to say, Iris?" Rose shot back. "Are you saying it looks like I planned to kill Cornell so I could move into his house? I didn't. It just worked out that way."

"It worked out the way you wanted it to work out," Iris snapped. "How can we believe you didn't have something to do with Cornell's death? You sure moved in fast on the Bird House. It doesn't look good at all."

"Cornell winding up dead didn't look good, no matter which way you slice it," Rose replied. "There's no way you can sugar-coat a man getting shot in the head. I might as well have the Bird House. If I stayed down here in the Main House, fretting and tiptoeing around, worrying about making it look good, it wouldn't bring Cornell back to life."

Iris made a face and turned away. "There's no point talking to you. You just aren't thinking clearly about this at all."

Violet intervened again. "All right. Both of you stop arguing. Iris, stop accusing Rose of planning to murder Cornell. It's not helping anything. If she had anything to do with Cornell's death, that's for the Sheriff to decide. Now, then. You changed the sheets on the bed in the Bird House. That's one less job we have to do. Now both of you come with me. There's the minister on the front porch now. We'll meet him downstairs and talk to him about what we want him to do."

The three sisters flew down the stairs and reached the front hall just as the minister's knuckles struck the door.

Violet opened it and greeted him with a casual smile.

"Good morning, Reverend," she sang out. "Please come in." He stepped into the hall. "I don't believe you've met my younger sisters. This is Iris, and this is Rose. This is Reverend Frederick Miles, from the United Lutheran Church in Butte."

The minister scanned the sisters from head to toe under pretense of bowing his tall, lean frame to them. "Good morning, ladies. It's a pleasure to make your acquaintance."

Rose and Iris returned his nod, and Rose noted his bushy beard and sandy mop of hair. He looked more like a Frontier cattle man than a minister, but everyone out West looked like that. A minister couldn't be much different from everyone else. He might even run a cattle herd of his own on the side, if he had some land to run them on.

"Now, Reverend," Violet began, "we have an unforeseen situation here. I'm sorry to tell you that our men aren't present at the moment. Sheriff Maitland deputized them at the last minute to help him track down an accused killer who went on the run in the area. So we don't have any men to marry just now, and we have no idea when they will be back."

The minister raised his shaggy eyebrows. "You don't say."

"My sisters and I just discussed the situation a moment ago," Violet continued. "If you are willing to wait just one day for the men to come back, we would like to put you up in a spare house we happen to have on the ranch. We'll do everything necessary to make you comfortable, and hopefully, we can go ahead with the wedding very soon."

"You see, Reverend," Iris added, "the man our men are after only left a few minutes before them, so they may return at any time. We wouldn't ask you to stay if we didn't think they would likely return before too long. We would greatly appreciate it if you would stay, as we're all anxious to celebrate this wedding as soon as possible."

The minister scratched his beard, and dust sprinkled out of it. "Well, let me see here. I don't really have anything pressing in Butte to go back for. I suppose I could stay."

Violet touched his sleeve. "Oh, thank you so much! I promise we won't keep you long. If this search looks likely to drag on, we'll let you go and celebrate the wedding at another time more convenient to you. You would be doing us a great service if you would stay."

The minister bobbed his shaggy head. "All right, Miss. I'll stick around at least until tomorrow, and we'll see what falls out." A wry smile spread across his face. "I gotta tell ya, I don't much mind a vacation in the country, if I do say so myself."

Violet and Iris returned his smile, and Violet bustled away

to show him up to the Bird House. Iris remained standing next to Rose in the hall.

"I guess he'll find out soon enough that only two of us are getting married," Iris remarked.

Rose gulped hard. "I could still be getting married. You never know what might happen."

Iris grimaced. "I know you're distraught about Jake running off to avoid arrest, but don't you think it's about time you faced the fact that he killed Cornell? You're not doing yourself any favors by continuing the illusion that he's innocent and that he'll clear his name. You're only making yourself more upset."

Rose's hands worked in and out of each other, and her eyes darted around the walls. "But he has to! He has to clear his name! How else can we get married?"

"You're not going to marry him," Iris insisted. "When are you going to get that through your head? You can't marry a killer."

"I have to marry him!" Rose whined. "I have to!"

Iris threw up her hands and turned away from Rose. "You're out of your mind. You've always been so level-headed in the past. I don't know what Jake's done to you to turn you into such a sniveling wreck. I just can't stand to talk to you anymore when you just keep repeating the same nonsense."

She spun away and stomped up the stairs, leaving Rose alone in her distracted despair.

Chapter 13

Rose retreated to her own room, but her dressing table mirror no longer held any sway over her. When she entered her bedroom, she cast one brief glance toward it and flung herself down on her bed.

How long would she have to wait here, on tenterhooks, before she knew whether the Sheriff had caught Jake? He might shoot Jake while attempting to capture him. What would she do then?

She sobbed into her pillow, already damp with tears, until she fell into a swoon of exhaustion.

She had no idea how much time elapsed before she woke up, but her restless anxiety tormented her more than ever. She took to pacing around the room, but before very long, she had no choice but to go out and roam the house.

Every place she turned repelled her. The clusters of daisies in the parlor, the cutlery and china laid out in the dining room for, even the open range outside every window plagued her beyond all endurance. They drove her onward to the next agonizing reminder of her loss.

The sun crept around the sky, hour dragged after painful hour, until Rose thought she would drop dead from the strain.

Once, she found herself near the back door and the path leading up to the Bird House.

She couldn't even go there anymore. The house only reminded her of her excitement at the prospect of going home to that house with Jake. Now the minister was up there, reading Cornell's books and drinking the tea Violet brought him. She couldn't even walk in the garden the way she used to. She fled from the sight of her lost future, around to the other side of the house, where she wouldn't see the Bird House anymore.

She came around to the front of the house and spotted Iris sitting in a rocking chair on the front porch. She would have walked away to avoid speaking to her. But at the same moment, Violet came out of the house, and all three sisters stood together, gazing toward the West, where their men rode in search of some elusive destiny.

"When do you think they'll come back?" Violet asked.

"It's impossible to say," Iris replied. "If they find him, they could come back any time. If they don't find him, it depends on how hard the Sheriff wants to keep pushing until they do find him. If the Sheriff wants to, he'll just keep driving them day and night until they find him and bring him in."

"Can he really do that?" Violet asked.

"He can do whatever he wants," Iris told her. "He's a lawman pursuing a wanted criminal. From what I saw, he's determined to bring Jake in. He didn't take Jake running off very well. He's made bringing him to justice a personal campaign. It wouldn't surprise me if he pushed on without stopping, and he'll take Chuck and Mick along with him."

Rose turned her face toward the range to hide her tears, and Violet touched her lips with her fingertips. "But this could take days, even weeks. When are we supposed to get married?"

"I guess we won't," Iris replied, "not until they catch Jake, at least."

The three sisters gazed westward again. The sun shone in their eyes, but none of them saw the scenery around them. All three saw only their men, riding somewhere out there. Were they riding toward their brides, or away from them?

The sound of horse's hooves disturbed the stillness of the moment, echoing out of the blinding sunlight, coming closer and getting steadily louder. The steady drumbeat of a galloping horse commanded all their attention.

Iris stood up from her rocking chair and shaded her eyes with her hand. Rose knit her hands together until her knuckles ached. Which one of them would it be?

The horse broke out of the canyon across the pasture and charged at full speed along the fence line toward the ranch house. Only when it reached the corner of the fence and skidded to a stop, unable to run any further, did the sisters see that its saddle was empty.

Rose gasped at the sight of the horse and started at a dead run toward the corner of the fence.

Violet stared. "But that's....!"

"That's right," Iris confirmed. "It's Jake's horse."

Violet and Iris hurried after Rose and came up to the fence after her.

The animal reared back, its eyes staring and saliva flying away from its foaming mouth. It ran back and forth in terror along the fence. Every time it came near the corner and saw the three women there, it ran off again.

Iris leaned over the fence and held her hand out to the horse. She called to it, and it settled down and swiveled its ears around. Finally, it snorted and shook its head before sidling up to her. The horse gave her hand a sniff and pretended to turn away in disgust before it abandoned the pretense and came close enough for her to catch hold of its bridle.

"What can have happened to Jake?" Rose asked.

"Anything could have happened to him," Iris answered.

"He could have fallen off, or he could be hiding out somewhere. He could have sent the horse back here in the hope that it wouldn't give him away. Anything could have happened."

"What should we do?" Violet asked.

"There's nothing to do," Iris replied. "When the Sheriff comes back, we can tell him the horse came home without Jake, but there's nothing we can do until then. The only thing to do is put the horse away in the barn."

"Will you do that, please?" Violet asked. "I have to go back to the house and talk to Rita about the food. We've got stacks of food for the wedding. I hope the men come back in time for supper tonight. Otherwise, it will all go to waste. It's a good thing the minister is here to help us eat it."

"You go ahead," Iris replied. "I'll put the horse away. He looks like he needs to cool down anyway. I'll walk him around the yard until he settles."

"I'll come with you," Rose told her.

Chapter 14

Iris stood at the corner of the fence, petting the horse and talking to it, until its breathing slowed and it stood quietly. Then she climbed over into the pasture and led the animal along the fence to the gate. Rose followed her, but the chance appearance of the horse confirmed her worst fears that Jake would never return.

"He looks like he's been running hard for a long time," Iris observed. "Something must have frightened him to make him run like that."

"Do you think…?" Rose trailed off.

Iris shook her head. "I'm sorry, darlin'. There's just no way to know right now. I know the uncertainty must be killing you, but there's just nothing more we can do but wait."

"I can't stand not knowing whether he's safe or not," Rose told her, "or whether he's gotten into a gun fight with the Sheriff and is bleeding his guts out in some forgotten corner of the frontier. I'd almost rather the Sheriff captures him and locks him up in jail. It sounds awful, but at least I would know he was safe. That's all I care about."

"I feel the same way about Mick," Iris replied, "so it must be ten times worse for you. Come on and help me put the horse away. That will help take your mind off things."

She led the horse into the barn yard and they circled the enclosure a few times to cool the horse down further.

"Being near him makes me think about being near Jake," Rose remarked. "I know he can't tell me where Jake is or what he's doing, but he knows. For some reason, being near him calms me down a little bit. I know it doesn't make sense, but that's the way I feel."

"It does make sense," Iris countered. "I would feel the same way, if this was Mick's horse. In a way, I feel the same way you do, even if it is Jake's horse. He's the only link we have to the men. I want to stay with him until the men come back."

Iris led the horse into the barn, tied him to a post, and removed his saddle. She started brushing his neck while the sweat-soaked square of hair on his back dried.

"Do we really have to tell the Sheriff the horse came back?" Rose asked. "Couldn't we just keep that to ourselves?" Rose caught Iris's eye. "Wouldn't you do that, just for me?"

Iris pressed her lips together. "I wouldn't do that, if I was you. The Sheriff already thinks you helped Jake plan to kill Cornell. You don't want to go casting even more suspicion on yourself if you can avoid it. And Violet and I wouldn't want to conspire to obstruct justice by helping keep it hidden."

Rose sighed. "I suppose you're right."

"Besides," Iris pointed out, "knowing the horse is here, that he came back without Jake, won't help the Sheriff find him. If anything, it will only make his job harder. A horse is a lot easier to find than a man on foot. A man can hide just about anywhere up in those mountains. You can spot a horse's tracks a mile off."

Rose brightened up. "Really?"

Iris smiled and nodded. "Without the horse, Jake could hide up there forever and never get caught. He may have sent the horse back for that very reason."

Rose blinked. "I didn't know that."

"Don't give up hope just yet," Iris told her. "You never know what could happen."

Iris finished brushing the horse and took a hoof pick from the nail on the wall. She bent down, lifted one of the horse's feet, and scraped the mud and stones out of the hoof with the point of the pick.

She cleaned one forefoot and then moved to the back legs, working her way around the horse in a circle. She slid her hand down the horse's rear leg and the animal raised its foot into her hand. Iris propped the hoof between her knees while she worked, but after one swipe with the hoof pick, she paused.

"Huh. That's funny," she muttered.

"What is?" Rose asked.

Iris hesitated. Then she continued cleaning out the horse's foot. "Nothing." She completed her circuit of the horse's legs and put the hoof pick away. "That's done. Let's put him up and go inside."

Iris led the animal into a stall, scooped him a measure of grain into his feed trough, and tossed him a flake of hay from the crib. She gave him one last pat on the neck, and she and Rose went out into the fading light of late afternoon.

They stopped on the front porch to gaze toward the range again. Rose sniffed. Iris rested a hand on her arm. "They'll be back soon."

"That's easy for you to say," Rose returned. "Your fiancé isn't under suspicion of murder."

"I just mean they'll bring him back safely," Iris corrected herself. "Everything will be all right. You've been saying so yourself for days. You should listen to yourself."

Rose blinked back her tears. "That was before Jake ran off. That was when I knew he wanted to marry me. I wish I could believe it now."

Iris gave her arm a squeeze. "Everything will be all right. Now come inside. You'll drive yourself crazy, staring that way."

Rose followed her inside, into the oppressive darkness of the house. The light coming through the windows faded to the pale purple of dusk. The three sisters moved though the rooms with the quiet reverence of church mice, hardly daring to speak above a whisper.

And still the men did not return. Rose sat at the window in the front parlor, unable to tear her eyes away from the western horizon. Her sisters exhorted her to lie down and rest or tried to engage her in conversation about anything unrelated to the disaster of Jake's disappearance. Nothing worked. Nothing could take her mind off of it. Nothing could mitigate the disaster of losing him.

She gave up and turned away from the window when full dark set in. There was nothing more to see out there. She would go upstairs and cry herself to sleep again—until tomorrow, when she would do the same thing all over again.

But just as she closed her eyes on the window, three riders barreled into the yard.

Chapter 15

The sisters met Chuck, Mick, and Sheriff Maitland in the hall.

"Did you find him?" Iris asked.

Mick shook his head. "We searched all over the canyon, the Bottom Run, and up on the table lands. We didn't even find his horse's tracks."

"That's because he's not on horseback," Iris told them. "His horse showed up here this afternoon with no rider. It looked half scared out of its wits."

"We'll go back out first thing tomorrow and keep searching," Sheriff Maitland declared. "He can't have gone far without a horse. He probably sent it back to cover his tracks."

"That's what I thought," Iris replied.

"There are any number of places he could be hiding if he doesn't have a horse," Mick remarked. "We won't likely find him at all."

"We'll keep looking anyway," Sheriff Maitland replied. "We won't stop until we find him."

The men exchanged glances with their brides, but no one said anything until Violet took charge. "You'll want to spend the night here, Sheriff. Let's figure out where to put you up.

Let me see here. The minister is in the Bird House, and these men are in the Fort House."

"Well, Hamilton's bunk is empty, isn't it?" the Sheriff replied. "I'll take that. If you have any objection, I'll sleep in the hay loft in the barn. Just about any place is good enough for me."

"I don't have any objection to you sleeping in Jake's bed in the Fort House," Violet assured him. "I can't imagine Chuck and Mick object, either. Do you?"

Chuck and Mick looked at each other. Then they shook their heads. "It doesn't matter," Mick replied, "just as long as we get some sleep. I'm worn out."

"Then come on into the dining room," Violet told them. "There's enough food to feed the Union Army in there. It's all left over from the wedding. You come, too, Sheriff. We need all the help we can get to eat it all."

The party moved into the dining room, and Violet fetched the minister from the Bird House to help eat the food intended for the wedding. The men ate while the women watched in silence. Rose gritted her teeth to stop herself from getting sick at the sight of them eating. If only Jake was here! He could eat a horse, no matter what the circumstances.

She wanted to flee to her room, but she had to wait long enough to make a polite departure. Thank the stars for Violet and Iris! They didn't eat, either, but just stared at their men in silent apprehension. The Sheriff and the minister devoured the roast beef and boiled pudding with gusto. Eventually, the conversation turned back to the search.

"Where will you look for this fugitive of yours tomorrow?" the minister asked.

"I suppose we'll look out on the upper flats of the mountain," Sheriff Maitland replied. "That's about the only place I can think we haven't looked already. We'll just have to be extra careful that we don't surprise him. He could do any desperate thing to avoid capture."

"Is he a very dangerous criminal?" Reverend Miles asked.

"I don't know anything about him, myself," Sheriff Maitland returned. "I've never even spoken to him, apart from the interview we had yesterday. But if he was cold-blooded enough to shoot Cornell Pollard three times, and that within hours of setting foot on this ranch, I reckon he'll stop at nothing to stay free. I reckon he's just about the most unscrupulous scoundrel I've ever dealt with."

Chuck and Mick exchanged glances with their brides, but Rose kept her eyes down, inspecting the woven fibers of the tablecloth. Did they care at all that this was her fiancé they were discussing so casually? The minister didn't even know the fugitive the Sheriff was describing was one of the men he came out to Rocking Horse Ranch to marry.

She waited a few more minutes before she excused herself and retired to her room for the night. She tossed around on her bed while the sounds of the house diminished and died away one after the other. Darkness covered the windows, and still she couldn't shed the tears burning in her eyes. Nervous energy kept her in a fever of dread.

The hours wiled away. Maybe she drifted off for a while. She couldn't tell. But sometime in the small hours, her door swung into the room, and a figure approached her bed. "Rose! Are you awake?"

"Iris!" Rose exclaimed. "What are you doing here?"

Iris sat down on the edge of the bed next to Rose's knees. "I've got to talk to you," she whispered. "There's something I've got to tell you. But we have to talk quietly. We can't let anyone hear us."

"What is it?" Rose asked.

"I know where Jake is," Iris breathed.

Chapter 16

"What?" Rose gasped. "How? How can you know where he is? The men said they searched all over the range and they didn't find him."

"I know where he is," Iris declared. "Do you remember when I cleaned out his horse's hooves?"

"Of course," Rose replied.

"I saw something in the horse's hooves that told me where Jake is," Iris told her.

"What was it?" Rose asked. "How can you be so sure?"

"You probably didn't notice it," Iris told her. "No one would notice who hadn't spent a lot of time out on that particular patch of country. That horse had a petal from a purple magnolia tree stuck in the dirt in its foot. There's only one tree like it growing anywhere around here. Wade Jackson pointed it out to me."

"But how can the men have missed him if he's on foot?" Rose asked.

"They wouldn't have known where to look," Iris replied. "That magnolia tree grows way up in one of the side canyons off the river. They wouldn't have been anywhere near it."

"So what are we going to do?" Rose studied Iris's outline in the dark. "I thought you wanted to tell the Sheriff everything you knew to keep yourself free from suspicion. You didn't tell him you knew where Jake was. Why didn't you?"

"We can wait until the men leave tomorrow morning," Iris replied. "Then we can go find him. But I'll only take you there on one condition."

"What is it?" Rose asked.

"You have to promise me," Iris continued, "that you'll convince Jake to turn himself in peacefully. We'll bring him back to the house so the minister can marry you. But after that, he has to agree, and you have to agree, that he'll go with the Sheriff without a fight. You're my sister, and I want to do what I can to help you marry the man you want to marry, but after that, he has to face the law without offering any resistance. Do you understand?"

"Oh, Iris!" Rose cried. "Thank you so much!"

"Keep your voice down!" Iris hissed. "You'll wake the living dead, carrying on like that!"

"Iris, you're a saint!" Rose breathed. "I agree to everything you ask. I can't tell you how grateful I am to you for this."

"Don't thank me," Iris returned. "I'm doing this as much for Mick as I am for you. I just can't stand the idea of these men getting into a gun fight bringing Jake in. Any of our men could get killed if that happens."

"I promise," Rose declared, "I'll do everything in my power to convince him to turn himself in. I want Jake back as much as anybody else. I can't bear the thought of him fighting with the Sheriff."

"All right," Iris replied. "Stay in your room and keep quiet. When the men come in to breakfast tomorrow morning, just stay in here and pretend to be distracted with grief. I'll meet the men in the dining room until they leave for the day. After we're sure they're good and gone, we'll leave."

"Thank you, Iris!" Rose exclaimed. "Thank you so much! I can't tell you how much this means to me."

Iris smiled and patted her on the leg. "You just did. I'll come and get you after the men leave tomorrow." She slipped out of the room as silently as she came.

The rest of the night passed in a ferment of excitement for Rose. If she dozed before Iris's visit, she never closed her eyes once afterwards. The moment she laid down on the bed, she bounced off of it and paced around the room. She checked the color of the sky outside her window a thousand times. When she found it still pitch black, she threw herself down on her bed and tried without success to sleep again.

The first glimmer of dawn brightened the sky only aggravated her more than ever. How long did it take three men to have breakfast? Weren't they supposed to be in hot pursuit of a dangerous fugitive? Why didn't they leave already?

At long last, the men sauntered out to the barn, got their horses saddled, and rode away. Rose watched them disappear into the horizon, only to find Iris at her side. "Let's go."

"Not just yet," Iris countered. "Just wait a little longer. We don't want them coming back and finding us gone."

"How long do we have to wait?" Rose grumbled.

"It's not just the men," Iris told her. "Violet and Rita are starting the weekend laundry in a little while. We should wait just long enough to make it look like we're disappearing to get out of work."

Rose giggled. "You think of everything, don't you?"

"I don't want to get caught," Iris argued, "and I don't want Violet getting in trouble, either. If we get caught, I want Violet to be able to claim in all honesty that she never knew we were gone. Violet is too good to get mixed up in this. She's defended you and Jake against all odds. We need to make sure she doesn't take any of the blame for helping either one of you."

"You're right," Rose admitted.

"I'll go down to the kitchen and find out what they're doing," Iris told her. "When they start boiling the water, I'll make myself scarce, and we can go. Then Violet won't see us riding away. She'll be too busy to look out the window."

She ducked out of the room, and Rose rested little bit easier knowing what she was waiting for. She expected Iris to come get her, so she jumped with surprise when she saw Iris crossing the yard toward the barn.

She turned around with her hand on the barn door and waved to Rose in her window, beckoning her to join her. Rose rushed down the stairs without even grabbing a shawl first. She paused on the lowest step just long enough to listen for Violet and Rita's voices in the kitchen. Then she snuck out and raced for the barn.

Chapter 17

In the dusty shadows of the barn, Rose found Iris saddling Jake's horse. "Why don't you get Paddy out?" Iris suggested.

"Can't we ride this one together?" Rose asked. "Why do we need two?"

"You and I can ride Jake's horse on the way out there," Iris reminded her, "but once we find Jake, he'll need another one to ride or he'll be walking back. Anyway, you can ride a horse as well as I can, so you might as well."

"True," Rose admitted.

"When was the last time you rode?" Iris asked. "It must be years. I can't remember the last time I saw you on the back of a horse."

"Neither can I, now that you mention it," Rose remarked.

"You used to be a terror when you were younger," Iris recalled. "You used to give Cornell grey hairs with your exploits."

Rose chuckled. "He worried about me a lot more than he worried about you, and look how that turned out."

Iris laughed along with her. "Now's your chance to put all that riding to good use. Now go get Paddy out and let's get out of here before someone starts to wonder where we are."

Rose saddled up Paddy, the Appaloosa gelding. "It really has been a long time," she told Iris. "I'd forgotten how relaxing and satisfying it is to work with horses."

Iris shot her a sidelong glance. "You look happier now than I've seen you in a long time. I've been worried about you for a while now."

"Maybe it's just the excitement of seeing Jake again," Rose suggested. "I've been beside myself ever since he took off."

"I don't think so," Iris argued. "You've been sitting in your room staring at the wall for months—years, in fact. Violet has noticed it, too. It isn't good for you. You need to get out and get some air once in a while."

Rose passed the cinch belt under Paddy's belly. "You're right. I guess I just expected that my life would change after I got married. I put all my hopes on moving out of the Main House and up to the Bird House. I thought my life would change when that happened, and I just sat there waiting until it did."

"No wonder you were so unhappy," Iris replied. "Anybody would be, thinking all their happiness was in the future instead of now."

"I never thought of myself as unhappy," Rose told her. "I was just waiting. I didn't think about now at all. I only ever thought about the future."

Iris shook her head. "Well, now is now, and you better deal with it now, otherwise it the future will never happen."

"I never really thought about it before," Rose repeated.

"Are you ready?" Iris asked.

"Yes," Rose answered. "Let's go."

The two sisters led their horses out the back door of the barn, where they couldn't be seen from the house. Then they swung up into their saddles. Iris kicked her heels hard against her horse's flanks, and he shot forward, across the pasture, toward the western ranges.

Without thinking, Rose did the same, and when Paddy rocketed after the other horse, Rose's heart leapt into her throat. She'd forgotten this part of horseback riding, too. The thrill of the horse's living flesh surging underneath her, the wind whipping her hair out of her face, and the ground falling away under the horse's pounding feet—how could she have lived all these years without this? What was life, without this exhilaration, this ecstasy?

She never envied Iris her work on the range until now. To think that Iris enjoyed this life-giving joy, the glory of the sun and wind and rain every day, all year round. And she, Rose, sat at her dressing table, staring and seeing nothing, experiencing nothing.

All these years, she scorned Iris for her rough, dirty life. In actual fact, it was her, Rose, who moldered away in a half-mummified death state in the back upper room of the house. Iris may have been dirty and her hands callused, but at least she was alive.

She wouldn't let this happen again. She would never go back to her dressing table mirror. No matter what happened with Jake, she would never settle for a life without the sun, the wind, horseflesh, work, and the company of her sisters and their families.

Iris kept her horse galloping full tilt across the open plane, but Rose caught up with her. She never restrained Paddy for an instant, but gave him all the rein his head would take. Sensing her eagerness, he stretched his neck forward and unleashed all his great energy in running. He drew up level with Jake's horse, and Rose urged him forward with her legs. He took her signal and pulled ahead of Iris's horse.

Rose laughed out loud, but the wind tore the sound out of her throat. The sound ringing up from her innermost soul combined laughing, singing, and flying. She never experienced anything like it.

Iris slowed to a walk when they reached the mouth of the

canyon, and Rose fell in at her side. Her cheeks flushed bright pink, and her black hair hung free on her shoulders.

Iris glanced sideways at her. "Are you okay?"

Rose nodded and smiled. "I forgot about this."

Iris cocked her head. "Which part?"

"I forgot what it felt like to ride so fast," Rose explained. "It's like flying. I forgot that."

Iris shook her head. "It's been way too long for you. I could understand Violet staying in the house and playing into Cornell's hands. In a way, she had no choice, but the job of managing the house always suited her. But not you. It never made sense for you."

"There was always Cornell," Rose pointed out.

Iris shook her head. "You never had any reason to lock yourself away. You didn't have to make Cornell happy. He always doted on you. You could have done whatever you wanted with him, and he would have been happy with it."

Rose examined Iris. "It must have been hard for you, the way you stood up to him all these years and did what he didn't want you to do. It must have been hard for you to be at odds with him for so long."

Iris turned away. "You have no idea how hard it was."

"I should have stood up for you against Cornell," Rose considered. "I'm sorry now that I didn't do more to help you."

"And I'm sorry," Iris replied, "that I said the things I did about you and Jake killing Cornell. Even if I believed that, I should have kept it to myself. I should have stood by you, whether you were guilty of it or not."

"Cornell wasn't a good man," Rose told her. "He wasn't the man we thought he was. He didn't deserve me getting along with him all these years. I shouldn't have been so concerned with getting along with him. I should have stood up to him the way you did. I should have stood with you when you argued with him."

Iris's eyes flew open. "Since when did you become so

down on Cornell? You never felt this way before."

"I only came to realize what he was really made of after he died," Rose told her. "I should have realized a long time ago that you and Violet were much more important than Cornell could ever be. I was foolish not to realize that."

Iris colored and held out her hand to Rose between their horses. "Let's make a pact right now that we won't let that kind of divide come between us again."

Rose grasped her hand, and the two sisters sealed their alliance with a smile.

Chapter 18

They walked steadily through the canyon with the growing daylight spreading down the walls of the cliffs above them. Golden eagles screeched overhead, and scrub jays croaked in the tree branches near their heads.

Rose turned her face up to the sky and let Paddy find his own footing through the forest litter and dead branches on the ground.

"It's awfully nice up here," she remarked.

"Do you know," Iris told her, "Pete and Wade camp up here and along the river when they tend the cattle in the summer. I always wished I could join them, but I couldn't risk Cornell finding out. Now Mick says we can come up here later in the summer and spend some time up here together. I can't wait!"

"That sounds wonderful," Rose exclaimed. "I envy you."

"You could come up here, too," Iris told her. "There's nothing stopping you."

Rose made a face. "Somehow I don't think that would go over very well with being a wife and mother."

"You're not a wife and mother yet," Iris pointed out. "Even if you marry Jake, you won't be a mother for a while. You'll have time to come out if you want to."

"I would love to," Rose exclaimed. "I wish I could."

"Why couldn't you?" Iris asked.

A shaft of sunlight broke through the canopy of treetops and flashed across Rose's face. "It would be so good for the soul, to spend time out here. I would love to. I wonder I never thought of it before."

Iris shook her head and chuckled. "You better be careful. You might get infected with the outdoors. You might find you couldn't live without it."

"I'm finding that out now," Rose remarked. "I don't know how I lived so long without it. I spent so much time outdoors when I was young. I thought then that I never would live without it. I don't know how I convinced myself to live so long indoors."

"The important thing is that you know better now," Iris replied. "You won't go back to staring at your dressing table mirror anymore."

"No, I won't," Rose declared.

They rode in silence for a while. Rose enjoyed the tranquility and beauty of the scenery so much she could almost forget what they were doing out there, miles from the ranch house, just her and Iris riding side by side through the hills.

Iris guided their horses up the main canyon along the river. Rose remembered every landmark and twist of the trail from her younger days of riding and exploring the range. She hadn't seen that country for years, but she greeted the rocks and bushes and ripples in the water as old friends. She loved them as if she hadn't been separated from them for more than a day or two.

Somewhere along the Bottom Run, Iris veered off the trail, and they started climbing up into a side canyon, up into the mountains. A little stream trickled along the floor of the canyon, and the horses tiptoed over rocks and tiny pools of crystal water.

After a while, Iris broke the silence. "We're getting close to the magnolia tree."

Rose caught her breath, and all the worry of the last few days flooded back. She kept her eyes on the trail ahead, searching every rock and tree root for any sign of Jake. Iris searched right and left, too.

"Do you think we ought to call out to him?" Rose asked.

"Let's get a little further along," Iris suggested. "He won't have become separated from his horse until after the magnolia tree. Let's wait until we get past it. He may be in an obvious place, or he may see us and come out to meet us."

They climbed a while longer until Iris pointed and said, "There."

A tree dripping with magenta flowers overhung the trail. Rose gasped in astonishment. She'd never seen any tree like it before. "How did that get here? It doesn't look like it belongs here at all."

"It doesn't," Iris replied. "Wade says someone must have planted it here, because it's the only one of its kind in the area. It can't have gotten way up here by accident."

"But who could have brought it? Who would plant it….here?" Rose glanced around at the scrub pine trees and rocky dry earth.

Iris shrugged. "We'll never know." She urged her horse forward.

Just above the magnolia tree, the trail took a sudden turn, jutting up through a crack in the cliff wall. Iris's horse stumbled on the fragile rock, and both horses shied away from the opening. Iris held her horse under tight control until he stopped stamping and stood still. She scanned the cliff face.

"He must be here somewhere," she remarked. "I can't see the horse going up there. For one thing, the trail isn't really wide enough to ride a horse any higher."

Rose looked around. "Where do you think he might be?"

"He could be anywhere," Iris replied.

A shout answered them from the other side of the narrow defile. Both women wheeled their horses around, and there, sitting at the base of a tree on the other side of the stream, was Jake.

Chapter 19

"Jake!" Rose slid down from her horse and jumped across the stream to him. She threw her arms around his neck and crushed him in her arms.

"What are you two doing here?" he asked.

Rose surveyed him. "Don't look so happy to see us. Why don't you get up and greet us properly?"

"I can't get up," Jake replied. "I sprained my ankle. I can't stand up."

"How did that happen?" Rose gasped.

"That horse," he jerked his head toward Iris's mount, "that horse threw me. A bird flew into his face and startled him. He threw me off and ran away. I landed on my foot, and I sprained my ankle. I can't stand up and I can't walk. That's why I've been sitting here since yesterday."

Rose looked down at his foot. "Are you sure it isn't broken?"

"It might be," he told her. "I can't stand on it, either way."

"Then it's just as well for you that we came," Rose replied. "We're here to take you back to the ranch. But you have to promise to turn yourself in to the Sheriff and let him take you back to Butte."

"Turn myself in?" Jake repeated. "Am I wanted?"

"Of course you're wanted," Iris shot back. "The Sheriff has been looking for you since yesterday morning to place you under arrest for Cornell's murder. You know that. He deputized Chuck and Mick to go looking for you."

"I didn't know anything about it," Jake snapped. "I didn't even know the Sheriff was at the ranch. If I had known he was looking for me, I never would have left."

Iris and Rose stared first at each other, then back at Jake. "If you didn't run from the Sheriff, why did you leave?" Rose asked.

"I told you," Jake declared. "I never even knew the Sheriff was at the ranch, let alone that he was looking to arrest me. After I left you at the Bird House, I decided to go for a ride up the canyon to clear my head before the wedding. I never saw the Sheriff, or Chuck or Mick, or anyone else after I left you."

Rose laughed in pure relief. "We all thought you ran off to avoid arrest."

Jake frowned. "I never would have run from the law. I never have, and I never will. If Sheriff Tom Maitland, or anyone else, wants to arrest me for Cornell's murder, or for any other thing, they can come and do it."

Rose felt tears falling down her cheeks. "I thought you didn't want to marry me. I thought you didn't want me to marry a fugitive."

Jake gaped at her. "You thought I ran away from marrying you? Never!"

Rose fell on her knees and threw her arms around him all over again, weeping on his shoulder and laughing for joy. Iris shifted from foot to foot in embarrassment.

"Anyway," Iris put in, "the Sheriff is looking for you and planning to arrest you and take you back to Butte when he finds you. Rose and I came out here to bring you back to the ranch to turn yourself in. You'll have to come with us."

"I don't plan on doing anything else," Jake shot back.

"The minister is at the house," Iris told him. "Maybe if you throw yourself on the mercy of the Sheriff, he might let you marry Rose before you leave."

"I won't throw myself on the mercy of the Sheriff," Jake growled, "but I'll do everything I can to get married before anyone hauls me away for Cornell's murder. You can bet on that."

"Then we all agree," Iris concluded. "Now we just have to find a way to get you back to the house."

"Can you ride?" Rose asked him. "If we got you onto a horse, do you think you could ride back?"

"I really don't know," Jake admitted. "I can't put any weight on this foot. Maybe if I took it at a slow walk I could do it."

Rose stood up. "Why don't you head back to the house, Iris? You've done enough, and you shouldn't run the risk of getting into trouble if you can avoid it. You might get home before Violet finishes the laundry, and no one will ever know you were gone."

"So what will you do?" Iris asked.

"I'll get Jake onto Paddy," Rose told her. "I'll walk him back slowly. It could take a while to get back. You should be home long before us."

Iris considered the situation. "All right. I'll go back ahead of you. But I think you'll need my help to get him onto Paddy's back."

Rose surveyed Jake's leg. "Okay. Thanks."

Rose got under one of Jake's arms, and between her and Iris, they managed to lift Jake up into a standing position on his good leg. Then he leaned on their shoulders and hopped over to Paddy. "Now what do we do?"

"I'll lock my fingers together," Rose told him. "You put your knee inside my hands, and I'll heave you up. This is the way we used to help each other get onto a horse's back when we were children learning to ride and couldn't reach the stirrups."

"We did that, too," Jake recalled.

"Good, then you know what to do," Rose replied. "You won't put any weight on your ankle. Then you can get up on his back. Just swing your other leg over."

Jake chuckled. "All right. Heave away."

Rose bent down and made a basket out of her woven fingers. Jake slid the knee of his injured leg into the basket, Rose heaved, and Jake swung his good leg over Paddy's back so he came to rest in the saddle.

Rose stood back and surveyed her work. "Good. That's fine. Now, get on your way, Iris. Get home as fast as you can, and carry on shirking the laundry work. If anyone asks, you don't know where I am and you haven't seen me since last night."

Iris stole a glance at her younger sister. "If I hadn't ridden up here with you today, I wouldn't know you were the same person I spoke to last night. You look different, your voice sounds different—everything about you is different."

"What's so different?" Rose asked. "I'm the same person."

"No," Iris replied. "You definitely are not the same person. You're someone I haven't seen in many years. You might even be someone I've never met before."

"Is it as bad as all that?" Rose asked.

"It isn't bad," Iris countered. "It isn't bad at all. I only wish I'd met this person years ago."

Chapter 20

After Iris rode away, Rose took Paddy by the bridle and led him down the canyon. Jake rode with one foot in the stirrup and the other dangling. They went at a fraction of the speed with which Rose and Iris rode up over the same terrain.

They picked their way between trees and around boulders for a long time without talking. Then Jake remarked, "She's right, you know."

Rose's head shot up. "Who? Right about what?"

"Iris," Jake told her. "She's right about you. You're different."

"Do you think so?" Rose put her head on one side, and then she turned back to watching her footsteps.

Jake nodded. "You're not the blinking wallflower you were just two days ago. I never saw a person change so dramatically in so short a time."

Rose snorted. "Blinking wallflower! Go on! I never was!"

Jake grinned. "I ought to know who I met at the hotel saloon in Butte, and this...." He scanned her up and down with eyes. "This is definitely not the same person."

Rose smiled to herself. "I didn't know what to think of you then. I only knew I had to have you. I never saw someone more fascinating that you."

"That just goes to show you really were a wallflower, if you though I was fascinating," Jake remarked. "I'm just a kid from the sticks."

"I didn't know what you were," Rose replied, "and I don't know what you are now. I only know you're mine. I know for certain, when I look at you, that we're meant for each other. Whatever the Sheriff does or says, we will be together."

"That's what you say," Jake returned. "We'll have to see how things work out."

"All I have to do," Rose insisted, "is to look at you and all my doubts disappear. I only worried after you left. Now that we're together again, I feel just as certain as ever that nothing can come between us."

"If we're going to be together," Jake maintained, "I think we ought to take this time to get to know each other again. If we're going to be married, it wouldn't do to marry a stranger."

Rose laughed at him. "Isn't that the point of marrying a mail-order bride? You're not supposed to know the person beforehand."

"I guess I feel differently now that I know you," Jake remarked.

"You just said you didn't know me," Rose shot back. "You said you wanted to get to know me. You're talking every which way."

"You're right," Jake admitted.

"So what do you want to know?" Rose asked. "Here I am. Get to know me."

Jake shook his head. "All I know is that you're different. What happened to you since yesterday?"

Rose thought it over. "I thought you ran away from me. I thought you didn't want to marry me if you were on the run or if you were under arrest. I thought you wanted me to remain free. All my hopes for our marriage and our life together came crashing down. I thought I might die from grief."

"I told you I didn't run away," Jake told her.

"But I didn't know that, and the Sheriff doesn't know it, either. He assumed you went on the run, and we all assumed the same thing." Rose shook her head. "It's gonna take a lot of explaining when we get back to the ranch."

"So what happened?" he asked.

"Yesterday," Rose continued, "Iris and Violet and I were standing on the porch when your horse came back with no rider. When Iris cleaned out his hoofs, she found one of those purple magnolia flowers in the dirt. She didn't say anything at the time. She only told me it wasn't a good idea to keep the horse coming home a secret from the Sheriff. Later that night, she came into my room and told me she knew where you were."

"So it was her idea to come and get me?" Jake asked.

"She made me promise," Rose told him, "that I would convince you to turn yourself in peacefully without a fight. She was worried about Mick getting hurt, if it came to a shoot-out between you and the Sheriff and the men. So we waited until they left this morning, and she brought me up here."

"That still doesn't explain why you changed so much." Jake examined her again. "I mean, look at you. You're unrecognizable. Your hair is down, and you're glowing. You look like some kind of angel."

"Angel!" Rose repeated. "My hair is black, and I've got mud all over the bottom of my dress."

Jake shook his head again. "I reckon there are black-haired angels, too. And as for the mud, well, that just completes the picture. So what happened to you?"

"Iris said we should bring two horses," Rose told him. "She said you would need something to ride, and it's been years since I rode. So I came on Paddy here. I'd forgotten what it felt like to ride a horse. I forgot how your legs become part of the horse's body, and the wind beats into your lungs and your skin, and you turn into something that doesn't belong to the earth anymore. You turn into some kind of four-legged bird."

Jake listened in silence.

"And it isn't even just the riding that does it," Rose continued. "Do you know what? Now that you tell me I changed, I can remember where I was and what I was doing when it started. I was brushing Paddy down and saddling and bridling him. Touching a horse, getting his smell in your nostrils and the dust in your eyes—it does something to the very fiber of your being."

"I know," Jake murmured.

"You know something else?" Rose went on. "I never even noticed these things when I was younger, when I was riding every day. I only noticed it now, after I've been locked in the attic of the house for years with no sun and no air and no dust. You don't realize how all those things make you alive, and without them, you aren't alive anymore."

Jake nodded. "I noticed that about you before. I noticed there was something missing from you. You were like a statue in a wax museum. You didn't talk, you didn't move, you hardly breathed. You didn't really even look alive. You look alive now."

The color mounted in Rose's cheeks and she shook her hair back from her face. The crisp clear air of the mountains bathed her face. "I feel alive. I feel more alive than I've ever felt before. I feel like I know what life is supposed to be like, and that I know what to do to make life worth living. I see my life stretched out before me, and it isn't the life I thought I would have when I first wrote to your about a mail-order marriage."

Chapter 21

"Is there room for me in your new life?" Jake asked.

"Of course!" Rose exclaimed. "There better be. I'm going to an awful lot of trouble to make sure of it."

"So what do you see us doing together in this new life of yours?" he asked.

Rose gazed at the green of the treetops against the blue sky, but images from her future passed before her eyes. "I see myself doing all the things I planned to do before, but there's another dimension to it. I see myself making a home for us in the Bird House, but when I see myself there, I don't act the same. I'm more…I don't know…more engaged, I guess."

"More alive?" Jake offered.

Rose smiled at him. "Exactly. I'm happier, more lively, and more loving to my children—and everyone else. Iris told me, when I was saddling Paddy, that she hadn't seen me so happy in a long time, but I didn't even realize I was unhappy."

"I didn't think you were unhappy," Jake remarked, "but I didn't think you were all that happy, either. Now, you look happy. Definitely happy. So keep talking. Keep telling me about your future."

"Look." Rose pointed to the corner where they approached the main canyon. "Here we are at the Bottom Run.

Iris told me the cowboys camp here in the summer when they come out tending the cattle."

"Mick told me the same thing," Jake replied. "It's a nice spot."

"Iris also said," Rose told him, "she and Mick plan to come out and camp here in the summer, just to get out of the house and spend some time together outdoors. It would be nice if you and I could do that, too."

"That does sound nice," Jake agreed. "There's just the little problem of the Sheriff wanting me for Cornell's murder. Have you forgotten about that?"

"I haven't forgotten," Rose replied. "But I'm more certain than ever that we can make him understand the situation. When you think about it, it really is a very small problem."

"Not so small, when you're the one accused," Jake countered.

Rose pierced him with her stare. "I *am* the one accused. You forget that."

"I haven't forgotten," Jake declared. "That's why I haven't pushed you to sacrifice yourself to protect me. But still, it's a problem we have to solve before we can go camping on the Bottom Run. Let's not get too far ahead of ourselves."

"I'm just telling you what I envision of our future life together," Rose told him. "I ought to tell you that, now that I've tasted the life outdoors again, I don't mean to give it up again. I'll spend a lot more time outside, riding horses and getting dirty the way I used to do when I was a girl." She laughed. "Those were the days! You should have seen me!"

Jake smiled. "I'd like to have seen you. That would be something to see."

"I'm telling you now," Rose repeated, "I won't give it up again. I won't go back to the way I was before. I won't be a wallflower in front of mirror."

"That's fine with me," Jake replied. "I'm more than

happy to see you tanned and windblown the way you are now. You look beautiful to me this way."

Rose blushed. "You've never said that before."

"We hardly talked before," Jake reminded her. "We've talked more in the last hour than we have in all the time since we first met."

Rose laughed, but looked away in embarrassment. Talking about talking stopped their conversation in midstream, and they strolled along the riverbank. Rose listened to the tinkle of the water over the stones and the voices of the birds. They whispered the sentiments of her heart more eloquently than she could express herself.

What was the point of talking, with these kindred all around her, revealing their wisdom and pointing her where she ought to go? She didn't have to make any decisions. She only needed to see these creatures and elements at their work to know her own purpose.

She slowed her pace as they reached the end of the canyon. Soon they'd be back at the house. It was only a matter of time before the Sheriff came back, and then he would want to take Jake back to Butte.

Could she handle the pressure? Would her new strength carry her through that confrontation? Would the life brimming inside her protect her and Jake from the Sheriff, or from any other adversary that came along?

She lapsed into a doubtful reverie, imagining all the possible scenarios that could unfold when they got back. She walked along blindly until her foot rolled off of a stick lying across her path.

In a flash, the stick whipped away from her with a hiss and a rattle, and Rose jumped back out of its way. The snake landed three feet away, rattling and thrashing and baring its fangs. Rose's sudden movement startled Paddy, who reared up on his hind legs, screeching and staring at the slender apparition of horror on the ground in front of him.

Unable to keep his seat with only one foot in the stirrup, Jake tumbled off the back of the horse and pitched head over heels over the grass. He crashed through a clump of brambles, and the thorns snagged on his shirt and tore the sleeve open.

The horse reared again, yanking the reins out of Rose's hands, and backed away. He probably would have bolted in the opposite direction, leaving them stranded, if Rose hadn't darted forward and seized the reins once more.

She glanced once back over her shoulder to make sure the snake was far enough away from them to pose no further threat. Indeed, she saw it slithering away into the grass. Paddy, on the other hand, refused to be pacified by reassuring words. He continued to rear and back away, staring all around him at imaginary foes.

Rose paid out the reins to their limit and let the horse move back, soothing him with her voice while keeping a firm hold on his reins. As she expected, he soon lost his fear and settled down. He finally allowed Rose to come close enough to pat him on the neck, and then she turned her attention to Jake.

"Are you all right?" she asked.

Jake sat up on the grass and brushed himself off. "I'm okay. That's a waste of a perfectly good shirt, but my head is intact. That's the important thing."

"You didn't injure your ankle any further, did you?" Rose asked.

Jake shook his head. "It's the same. But now I've got to get back on the horse, and we don't have Iris to help us."

"I think I can manage. Here, lean on me." She propped herself under one of his armpits and hoisted him up so he balanced on his good foot. "Now, hop over and I'll give you a boost up into the saddle the way I did before."

Chapter 22

Jake followed her instructions, but when he hopped over next to Paddy, the horse shied away again and refused to stand still.

"Blasted horse!" Jake cursed under his breath.

"Settle down," Rose told him. "I'll handle him."

"Settle down!" Jake spat. "Don't talk to me the way you talk to that animal. I'm not your pet."

Rose's eyes flew open is surprise. Then she laughed in his face. "You're my precious pet, darling." She patted him on the shoulder. "Now, come here. Hold onto this branch and balance yourself while I tie him up."

Jake grumbled, "Blasted horse!" But he did as she said.

Rose laughed again. "There's no point getting mad at him. He's just an animal. He's had a bad scare, and he doesn't understand what's going on. Give him a break."

Jake shot her a quick look and shook his head.

"What?" she asked.

"You," he said.

"What?" she asked again. "What about me?"

"Just you." He waved his hand toward her. "The way you're talking. The way you're acting. The way you handled that horse just now. I wouldn't have recognized you. I bet your own sisters wouldn't recognize you now."

Rose stopped and thought. "You're right. I'm more than I thought I was." She threw back her head and laughed in pure exuberance at the vital energy pulsing through her. She raised her arms to the sky. "I love this! I never thought it would be like this."

Jake chuckled at her and shook his head.

Rose tied Paddy by the reins to a tree and swung his body around so his flank touched the trunk. Then she supported Jake while he hopped over. This time, when he approached, Paddy couldn't back away and Jake grasped the saddle horn.

But instead of waiting for her to boost him up into the saddle, he snaked his arm around her waist and pulled her against him.

She gasped aloud. "Hey? What are you doing?"

"Are you still mine?" he breathed.

She tried to laugh him off. "Whose else would I be? You've only been gone a day."

He leaned closer and brushed his moustache against her cheek. "You haven't decided to sell me down the river to the Sheriff?"

"Sell you down the river!" Rose guffawed. "How could I do that? Oh, how you do go on! I'm bringing you back to the ranch so I can marry you. Remember?"

Jake ignored her. "Rose?"

Rose sighed, and her body relaxed against him. His fingertips dug into the hollow under her ribs and a rain of sparks crackled down the backs of her legs. Her knees almost buckled underneath her.

"Rose?" Jake growled, but his voice didn't want any answer.

Her eyelids slid closed, and her head lolled back under the pressure of his bristled upper lip on her cheek. Her breath caught in her throat as his lips slid down over her jaw line to her neck.

Then her knees really did fail. She would have toppled onto the grass if he hadn't held her around the back.

"Rose," Jake rumbled, sliding down to her collar bone.

He let his legs buckle under him, and he fell on top of her on the soft grass, but she didn't notice. She only knew they were merging into each other, falling through the center of the earth and out the other side into heavenly ether.

His hands tugged at her dress and roamed around her waist to the front of her ribs. Rose struggled to breathe, and her body dissolved into nectar. Jake sipped the pearls of nectar from behind her ear and under her chin.

He said something, but she didn't hear him. Flashes of light blinded her eyes, and the explosions blocked her ears.

"Rose?" he asked.

"What are you doing to me?" she panted.

"We're in the middle of the trail, you know," he pointed out.

"Huh?" Rose blinked her eyes, and the blue sky took the place of the flashing stars.

"We're in the middle of the trail," he told her. "If the Sheriff and the men come along, they'll run right into us. We should move."

"Oh. Right." Rose swallowed. Her voice rasped in her parched throat. "I guess we should....move."

Jake pushed himself back and gazed into her eyes. "Are you all right?"

Rose nodded. Her voice wouldn't work. Was that the end of it? The Sheriff might come, so that's the end. See you in the springtime.

"Let me help you up." Jake moved over on the grass and pulled her up by the hand. Rose sat up and her hair fell down around her face and over her eyes. She'd forgotten her hair was down. She didn't have any idea what she looked like.

What was she doing, rolling on the ground with a man she

wasn't married to? Who was this reckless siren she'd turned into?

Confusion clouded her mind. She jumped to her feet and would have run away—but where?—if Jake hadn't called to her, "I'll need you to help me mount up."

She spun around and saw him still sitting on the ground. She shook her head and the hair danced in front of her eyes. "Right. Sorry. I forgot."

Jake chuckled. "Are you sure you're all right? Are you ready to go back to the house, or do you want to go sit somewhere and pull yourself together? We don't have to head straight back. The Sheriff won't find me until we get back."

Rose shook her head again, but it did nothing to organize her thoughts. "No, we can go back. I'm fine. At least, I will be fine once we start moving. I'm just a little…flustered."

She got under his arm and propelled him onto his one good foot. He hopped over to Paddy, who still stood placidly tied to his tree. What Paddy must have thought at the sight of them lying on the ground together! Thank heaven he couldn't tell anybody!

Rose laced her fingers together and boosted Jake into the saddle. They didn't try to talk to each other again, and Rose took Paddy's bridle and led him the rest of the way back to the ranch.

Chapter 23

At the opening of the canyon, Jake took hold of Paddy's reins and pulled the horse to a stop. Rose looked up at him to see what he wanted, and he slid down. He landed gingerly on his good foot and, holding onto the saddle horn, he hopped around to face Rose.

He cast a glance across the pasture. The barn, the Main House, the Fort House, and the yard lay spread out in front of them like a miniature child's barnyard. The late afternoon sun glinted off the windows of the Bird House, perched on the far hill.

Jake and Rose looked across the landscape.

"Are you ready to go back and face the music?" Rose asked. "It's been nice out here, free from all the cares of the ranch."

Jake caught her around the waist again. He pulled her against him and kissed her. "Are you still mine?"

"Always," Rose whispered. "Always yours. No matter what happens."

Jake planted one more kiss on her lips and let her go. "Then I'm ready to go back. As long as you're mine, I can face anything."

She helped him up again, and they ambled down to the barn.

No one came out to meet them.

Rose peered around the yard. "I wonder why no one has come out."

"Maybe they're busy," Jake suggested. "Or maybe they're hiding."

Rose chuckled. "I'll drop you off on the front porch. Sit in the rocker while I put Paddy away. Then I'll help you inside. The Sheriff can't be here yet, or he'd be out here like a shot."

Jake followed her orders, and she found him in the rocker when she came up from the barn.

"Come on inside and sit down in the front parlor," she told him. "I'll get you something to eat. You must be hungry."

"I'm starving," he replied.

She deposited him in the window seat by the front window and fetched him a board with a few slabs of bread and cheese and dry sausage from the kitchen. She sat next to him while he ate it.

"What do you want to do when the Sheriff comes in?" she asked.

Jake shrugged. "Start talkin'. Start talkin' fast. That's all I can do. I hope to high heaven he waits long enough to listen."

Rose shuddered. "He doesn't seem like the waiting type."

"No," Jake agreed. "I noticed that, too. We can only try. We've left the explanations a little too late."

"I'm sorry about that," Rose replied.

"It doesn't matter now." Jake nodded toward the window. "Here he comes now."

Rose jumped out of her seat just in time to see the three riders thundering into the yard. Chuck Ahern and Mick McAllister followed Sheriff Maitland to the barn, and in another minute, all three burst through the front door. Violet and Iris flew down the stairs and met them in the hall.

A single glance through the open parlor door showed them Jake Hamilton, the blood-thirsty fugitive they'd hunted for two days, leaning on his fiancé's arm in front of the window seat.

"You!" the Sheriff snarled. "You—*here!*"

"I'm here, Sheriff," Jake declared. "You don't need to look for me. I'm right here."

"Well," the Sheriff boomed, "I'm here to tell you that you're under arrest for the murder of Cornell Pollard. You're coming back to Butte with me."

"Yeah." Jake glanced at Rose. "I heard you were lookin' to arrest me, and I'll go with you. I won't put up any resistance."

"What did you run for, then?" Sheriff Maitland shot back.

"I didn't run. I explained to these ladies here," he indicated Rose and Iris, "that I didn't even know you were here, let alone looking for me. I went out for a ride to clear my head before the wedding, and I got thrown from my horse and sprained my ankle. The horse took off and left me sitting under a tree. I wouldn't be here now if they hadn't come and got me."

Sheriff Maitland scowled at him. "And you expect me to believe that story?"

"You believe whatever you want. That's the truth. I've never run from the law, and I wouldn't start now. I've got nothin' to fear from you or anyone else. If I knew you wanted to arrest me, I would have come straight to ya." Jake turned to Rose. "It looks like he isn't going to listen."

The Sheriff stepped forward and pointed. "What is that?"

Jake glanced down at the side of his arm where the torn fabric of the shirt left his skin exposed. A ragged gash encrusted with dried blood marred the smooth contours of his upper arm. "This? I fell and hurt myself."

"He said he fell of his horse," Iris reminded the Sheriff.

"That didn't happen today or even yesterday," Sheriff Maitland retorted. "Look at it. It's all scabbed over and sealed tight. That wound is a couple a' days old, at least."

"That could have happened anywhere," Mick put in. "What does a cut on the arm have to do with murder?"

Sheriff Maitland straightened up. "Never mind. You're goin' back to Butte. You can tell your whole story to the jury."

Jake squared his shoulders. "Sheriff, you might think I'm guilty of killing Cornell, and I wouldn't blame you if you did. But I never ran from you or tried to avoid arrest, and you have my word of honor on that. I'll go to Butte with you without a fight. I only ask one favor, and that is that you let me marry this lady here before we go. It'll only take a minute. The minister is right here at the house. I swear to you, on my honor, that I won't try to escape."

The Sheriff squinted at him and pursed his lips. "I don't like you, Hamilton, and I thought you were guilty from the minute I first met you. But I believe you didn't try to run away, and I don't see any reason to punish the lady for your misdeeds. I'll stick around until you can marry her, but I'm not letting you out of my sight for one minute. I'll wait while the ladies change into their wedding dresses, but you can forget about wearing anything other than the clothes on your back."

Jake smiled. "That's just fine with me. I don't want to wear anything else. As long as I leave here as Rose's husband, I'll be satisfied and I'll cooperate with everything you want me to do."

Sheriff Maitland turned his gaze on the three sisters. "You ladies had best get changed. I'll give you all one hour to get this wedding over with, and then we're headin' out."

Chapter 24

The three sisters exploded into a flurry of activity.

"I'll run up to the Bird House and get the minister," Iris announced.

"You men," Violet ordered Chuck and Mick, "get up to the Fort House and change your clothes. When you're done, come down to the back parlor and we'll meet you there."

Everyone split off in different directions, leaving Jake and the Sheriff face to face in the hall.

Rose bumped into Violet on the upper landing at the top of the stairs.

"Would you still like me to help you get dressed?" Violet offered.

"I suppose you'll get hurt if I say no," Rose remarked, "so you might as well."

Violet smiled at that. "All right. I'll come with you."

In her room, Rose ignored her mirror and they both turned their attention to the gown Violet made her. It lay spread out on the bed where Violet left it that morning.

"I'm glad you decided to wear it," Violet exclaimed. "I think you're going to make a magnificent bride in that dress."

Rose sighed. "If you say so."

"You always were the prettiest of the three of us."

"I am not," Rose retorted. "You and Iris are just as pretty as me."

"You don't have to say that," Violet replied. "You know you are. Iris is too weathered now from her years on the range to ever be truly pretty again. That Mick McAllister is a saint for loving her the way he does. He doesn't see her appearance at all. He only sees the woman she is on the inside, the woman who saved this ranch from ruin."

"She isn't weathered," Rose argued. "She just has a little bit of color in her face from being out in the sun. That will fade once she's spent a few years indoors."

"And I'm practically an old maid," Violet continued. "I'm too old to make a really beautiful bride. And I've had too much care myself these last few years. I suppose it shows in my face."

"Now I know you're talking nonsense," Rose shot back. "You're only twenty-three. You're hardly an old maid. And if you're showing the care of the last few years, then the next few years being married to your sweetheart and sharing the upkeep of the ranch with the rest of us should clear your face again. You'll be glowing in no time, and I'm certain you'll be glowing when you stand before the minister downstairs."

"I hope you're right." Violet tied the strings. "Now sit down and let me do your hair."

Rose took her seat in front of the dressing table, but she kept her eyes cast down into her lap so she wouldn't see her reflection. She wanted to preserve the memory of the life and love she felt up in the canyons. The new Rose would marry Jake. That stranger from yesterday morning, the stranger she saw staring back at her all these long, weary months—she wouldn't marry Jake, and she wouldn't live in the Bird House—*her* house. That was reserved for her shining dream.

She didn't watch or even notice what Violet did with her hair. She only heard Violet speaking to her as from an immeasurable distance.

"There," Violet exclaimed. "You look lovely. What a treasure Jake is getting! If he only knew the half of it."

Did Violet really believe that? Violet loved Rose and Iris like a mother. She didn't see their faults, and she could never believe anything bad about them. She couldn't believe Rose had anything to do with Cornell's death is she told her point blank it was true.

Maybe Violet believed Jake killed Cornell, but she took the same maternal view of the three mail-order grooms as well. She already knew Chuck and Mick were innocent, and she just couldn't get her head around to believing Jake shot Cornell within hours of arriving at Rocking Horse Ranch.

The whole scenario did seem far-fetched, when Rose thought about it. It just didn't make sense. So why should anyone jump to believe it?

Violet didn't seem to notice any transformation in Rose, either. She didn't seem to notice Rose had even left the ranch. She wasn't capable of seeing anything in anybody except goodness.

"Chuck is getting a prize in you, too, Violet," Rose told her. "You'd make anyone a wonderful wife, and you're going to be a wonderful mother, too."

Violet blushed. "That's nice of you to say, darlin'. I've always done my best."

"You've been like a mother to me since Mama died," Rose went on. "I'm glad I had you around, because as much as Cornell tried to be everything to us, he couldn't be a mother. He couldn't take the place of an older female in my life. You've always held that place for me."

"I'm hardly an older female," Violet told her. "I'm only four and a half years older than you. I couldn't be a mother to you, although I wish I could have been. Losing Mama was particularly hard on you. I understand that."

"You did a fine job," Rose replied. "You did what no one could ever do, and I feel it right now, with you getting me ready for my wedding. You're the only one who could, and I wouldn't want anyone else here right now."

Rose heard a sniff and stole a peek at her sister in the mirror, only to see Violet wiping her eyes.

"I don't know what's wrong with me," Violet blubbered. "I just don't seem able to stop crying at the drop of a hat."

Rose turned around on her stool and took Violet's hand. "Cornell's death really hit you hard, maybe harder than even you realize. You've worked all these years to stay on good terms with him, and then to fall out with him so terribly right before you find him dead—it must be hard for you."

"Not as hard as you, I'd say," Violet returned. "I think you may be denying how much Cornell's death affected you. That's why you're acting the way you have been. I think the shock will hit you later on. You don't feel it now, but it's coming out in subtle ways, and you don't realize it. I think Iris doesn't realize it, either. That's why she thinks you're acting guilty of killing him. You have to forgive her for that."

Rose compressed her lips. "Iris can think whatever she wants."

"Listen to me," Violet maintained. "She knows as well as I do that you didn't have anything to do with Cornell's death. She just doesn't understand how you could be acting so callously. She doesn't realize you're burying your feelings about him behind a hard exterior. She'll understand later, when you start expressing your feelings more openly."

"I won't ever express any feeling for Cornell because I don't feel anything for him," Rose insisted. "He's dead. He's gone. I'm just glad I'm moving into the Bird House. And I'm glad I'm marrying Jake. I won't change my mind about that."

"That's what you think now," Violet told her. "You'll see I'm right."

Rose sighed. "Okay, Violet. I won't argue with you anymore."

"Your hair's finished," Violet told her. "Are you ready to put your dress on now?"

Rose cast a look toward the bed. "All right. I guess so."

"You don't have to wear it if you don't want to," Violet insisted. "I'll understand if you don't."

Rose grimaced. "No, you won't. But you will soon."

Chapter 25

Rose went to the bed and lifted up the dress. It really was the most beautiful wedding dress she'd ever seen. It was much nicer than anything they could have ordered professionally made from San Francisco or Chicago or Denver. And every stitch in it bore Violet's loving fingerprints. That made it all the more beautiful and valuable.

Maybe one day, her daughter would wear this dress to get married. Maybe it would be handed down from mother to daughter for a hundred years. She couldn't well start off a tradition like that by not wearing it, could she?

Imagine the story her descendents would tell! "Great-grandma Rose had this dress, but she didn't wear it for her wedding." No, that would cast a shadow over every other wedding held in her family. Anyone who wore the dress would carry the stigma she cast on it.

She let Violet unbutton her soiled dress. She shucked it off and changed into the underwear Violet made to go under the wedding dress. All the time, she kept Violet strategically positioned to one side of her.

Violet took hold of her corset strings and tugged on them. Rose gasped between yanks on the strings. Finally, she picked up the dress.

She opened the back and stepped into it. She pulled the top of it up around her shoulders and slid her arms into the sleeves. She arranged the skirts around her legs. Then she stood with her back to her sister while Violet fastened the long row of buttons up her back.

She turned around and looked at herself in the glass. "It really is wonderful. I don't think I've ever told you how much it means to me that you made it for me. It's the greatest blessing you could bestow on my marriage. Thank you. This dress means the world to me."

Violet sobbed behind her. "You are so welcome! I'm so happy to see you wearing it."

"I'm sorry I ever gave you any reason to doubt that I would," Rose replied. "It was heartless of me."

"That's okay," Violet returned. "Seeing you in it now makes up for everything. And seeing you standing before the minister in it is all the reward I could hope for. I'm so happy you're marrying someone you love, and who loves you in return."

"I am," Rose assured her. "You shouldn't listen to Iris about Jake being guilty of Cornell's murder. If you only knew what a wonderful, kind, gentle man he is, you'd both know he couldn't do anything like this."

"We just want what's best for you," Violet insisted. "We only worry about you marrying Cornell's killer because we care about you."

"I understand that," Rose replied. "But you have to believe me. I'm not marrying Cornell's killer."

"Are you absolutely certain of that?" Violet asked.

"I've never been more certain of anything," Rose declared.

"If you say so, I believe you," Violet told her. "Now quick! Give me a hug, because I have to go change my clothes and get myself ready. Oh, I must look a mess! I hate to think of Chuck seeing me like this. I must look like a lobster." She blew her nose on the corner of her apron.

"You look as beautiful as ever, even in your old work dress." Rose reached out her arms to embrace her sister, and as she did so, the ruffles of her sleeves fell back, exposing the delicate white flesh of her forearms.

Violet let out a gasp. "What's that?"

Rose's heart sank, but she couldn't back out now. She held up her forearm to reveal a bright purple bruise slashing across the milky white canvas of her arm. "That's why I didn't want to wear your dress."

Violet's mouth flew open. "But how did you get it? Oh, it looks terrible! Is it painful?"

"Not really," Rose replied. "Sometimes, when I grip something very tightly, it aches a little, but not too much."

"Where did you get it?" Violet asked again.

"I just fell down and hurt myself," Rose told her. "It's nothing. But now you understand why I didn't want to wear the dress. I didn't want anyone to see it."

"Oh, of course!" Violet laughed hysterically. "Oh, darlin', I'm so glad you told me. That explains everything."

She threw her arms around Rose's neck and ran out of the room, laughing and crying at the same time.

Rose sank down onto her stool with her back to her mirror. The first domino had fallen. All the others couldn't be long in falling, too. Then what? She took a deep breath. She could only ride out the storm and see it to its end.

She sat still for as long as she dared. She only stirred when the sound of voices roused her from out on the landing. The moment had finally arrived. Rose picked up her veil from the bed and tried to drape it over her own head. But the angle didn't work. She couldn't attach the pins to her hair without seeing them from the back.

Maybe she could get Violet to do it before Jake saw her in the parlor. She ducked out of the room with the veil in her hand. Sure enough, she ran into Violet and Iris on the landing. They stood at the head of the stairs, just ready to descend.

They both wore their own wedding dresses with their veils hanging over their faces. Violet held a bouquet of ox-eye daisies in one hand.

"Oh, thank goodness you're here!" Violet exclaimed. "We were hoping we would meet you when you came out and we could all go down together."

"Here I am." Rose held out her veil. "Could you put this on for me?"

Violet's eyes flew open. "Oh! I forgot." She gave Rose her bouquet to hold and pinned the veil on. Then she lowered it over Rose's face. "By the way, I have something for you." She went back into her room.

When she came out, she held out another bouquet to Rose. Sprigs of deep green pine needles surrounded white rose buds. Rose's mouth dropped open. "Where did you get these?"

Violet smiled. "In the Bird House garden. Didn't you know Cornell had roses up there? You might not have seen them. They're around the back of the house."

Rose's eyes welled up with tears. "You didn't have to do this. After the way I've treated you, you shouldn't have."

Violet blinked her own tears away. "You haven't done anything other than what anyone else in your situation would have done. Think of this as my wedding gift to you. I didn't think you'd make yourself a bouquet, and no bride should be without one. Look, Iris has one I made for her, too."

Iris held up a bouquet of creamy pink day lilies.

"I couldn't find any irises at this time of year," Violet told her, "but she seems to like it, and the color matches the trim I used in her dress, so it all works out in the end."

Rose brushed her tears away on the ruffle of her sleeve. "You're an angel, Violet. None of us deserves the work you've done for us all these years. It's going to be hard living away from you after I've depended on you for so long."

"Nonsense!" Violet tried to smile through her tears, but her mouth only screwed up into a sob. "You'll be more than happy to get away from me and run your own house for a change."

Rose shook her head. "I don't know what I'll do with myself. I'll never sleep alone ever again. I'll never wake up alone again. And I'll never sleep or wake up in the Main House again."

Violet and Iris stared at her, but she couldn't stop her words flooding out. "You know what I wish? I wish Mama and Papa were here right now. I'd like to say good-bye to them right now."

"But they've been dead for years," Violet pointed. "We said good-bye to them a long time ago."

"Maybe you did," Rose corrected her, "but I didn't. I never realized back then that I needed to say good-bye. I don't think I ever even realized they were gone until right now. Now I'm saying good-bye to my childhood home and to my childhood. It only seems appropriate to say good-bye to them, too."

Violet wept openly. "Oh, how you do go on!"

"Come here and hug me." Rose reached out for her sisters. "Let's promise right now that we won't say good-bye, not today or ever. Promise me you'll both be my sisters forever, and we'll always live together and annoy each other just as much as we do now. I can't face marrying Jake if we don't promise."

They all embraced at once and sobbed into each other's veils. Eventually, they pushed each other away.

"Now, come on," Violet sniffed. "Pull yourselves together, girls. We've got three men and the minister waiting for us downstairs. We can't wait any longer. We can say more good-byes—I mean, *not* good-byes—when we get ready to go home to our own houses. My word, it's going to be awfully quiet around here without you two in the house." She laughed and cried all over again.

They composed themselves as best they could and then the three white apparitions floated down the stairs.

Chapter 26

They tiptoed down the hall in descending order of age and glided into the parlor. The minister stood at the far end of the room, facing the door. Chuck and Mick stood to one side of the minister, and Jake sat in a chair against the wall. Sheriff Maitland hung back in a corner of the room with his legs planted wide apart and his hands clasped behind his back.

Mick stood next to the minister, dwarfing him by a head, and fidgeting uncomfortably in a stiff wool suit of charcoal grey. His eyes latched onto Iris the moment she stepped into the room, but he didn't smile or blush or shift around the way he did during the past days. He froze stiff, unable to tear his eyes away from her.

Then came Chuck in a brand new black tuxedo. He flushed with happiness when his eyes met Violet's through her veil, and he smiled the same delighted smile he wore ever since he met her at the Butte train station.

Jake struck a curious contrast to his fellow mail-order grooms in his dusty trail clothes, hat, boots, and gun belt. When Rose entered the room, his eyes locked onto her and wouldn't let her go. Her heart pattered at the sight of him. She almost ran into the side table when she couldn't take her eyes off him to pay attention to where she was going.

So this was it. She was going to marry him after all. All her hopes, dreams, and anxieties swirled together in a giant wave that crested and threatened to break over the top of her. Oh, please, please let it be me, she thought. Let it be the Rose from today that marries him, the Rose that brought him home, the Rose that led his horse by the bridle, the Rose that lay with him underneath the trees. As long as that Rose marries him, the rest will take care of itself. Let that be me. Let me be that Rose from now on.

The minister smiled on them all in a paternal way. He waved the brides toward the opposite side of the room. He didn't need to bother, because Violet led them there. They lined up like batters on a baseball diamond. Rose would have laughed at the thought, but Jake's stare kept her silent.

The minister began his lecture, "We are gathered here today...."

The Sheriff vanished into the wallpaper.

Rose saw only Jake's glinting black eyes across the room and heard only the hammering of her own heart. The blood rushing to her face blinded her to everything else. How could anyone hear the minister with that deafening roar filling the room? Would she hear him asking her if she took Jake for her husband?

She managed to tune in just long enough to hear the minister explaining the duties and obligations of husband and wife. How could he know? How could he know what passed between her and Jake? How could he know what their marriage would build itself on?

He couldn't. What he said didn't mean a thing. No one could ever know or understand. Maybe what passed between them never happened before in the history of the world.

Finally, the minister wound up his interminable lecture. Somewhere in there, he asked if anyone knew any reason why this marriage should not take place, but no one said anything. No one mentioned anybody being guilty of Cornell's murder.

All that bluster fell by the wayside.

Then the minister glanced sheepishly around the room. "So who's going first?"

The three grooms looked at each other, and the three brides looked at each other.

"I'm the oldest." Violet stepped out of line into the middle of the room. "I'll go first."

Chuck stepped out of line to meet her with a grin stretching from one ear to the other. He couldn't stop himself from laughing, but his eyes brimmed with tears. From behind her, Rose saw Violet's shoulders shaking with laughter and sobs. She didn't need to see the inexpressible joy on Violet's face. There it was, in full view, on Chuck's face looking at Violet.

Then began the vows. "Do you, Charles, take this woman, Violet, to be your lawfully wedded wife? To love, honor, and cherish, forsaking all others, for better or for worse, in sickness and in health, 'til death do you part?"

Did he really have to ask? Anyone looking at Chuck would know he did, and gladly. His voice cracked when he said, "I do," so the words barely came out at all. He didn't have to say anything. And Violet? Did she take this man, Charles, to be her lawfully wedded husband? No woman ever took a man as her husband more joyfully, more gratefully. And no woman ever intended to love, honor, and obey with more sincerity than Violet.

Rose heard her sobs when Violet said, "I do." Rose sniffed back her own tears for Violet's happiness. No one deserved happiness more than Violet. No one had sacrificed more. No one dedicated more effort to the happiness of others and lost more sleep in her anxiety to keep them all tied together as a family.

She'd earned the most exquisite happiness for herself. She'd earned a family with a good, solid man at her side, and she'd earned the Main House as her home. Rose didn't envy

Violet one bit. She only wished she could do something to contribute to Violet's happiness.

But she couldn't. Violet remained the sole architect of her own destiny. Under her anxious, fluttery exterior beat the heart of a stalwart. Violet would never give an inch when she knew what was right. She would never flinch on something she knew she deserved. She would never waver in her single-minded determination to get it, and she built an empire of goodness around her in the process.

In spite of her own assurances to her sisters upstairs, Rose grieved the loss of Violet from her own life. Violet would never be her surrogate mother again. She would move to the Bird House, and Violet would become Chuck's wife and the mother of children. They would never be the sisters they had been up until this very moment.

Rose glanced around the room and saw everyone else in tears, too—everyone but Jake. Mick and Iris watched Chuck and Violet exchange vows with tears of joy streaming down their cheeks. Rose never saw Mick so emotional before. He stared at the newlyweds as if he couldn't believe such happiness existed in the world, as if he didn't believe marrying Iris would bring him the same joy.

Iris sobbed at Rose's side. No doubt she felt the same loss at moving out of her childhood home. The minister sniffed between passages of his service. Didn't he see this kind of love and joy all the time? Were Chuck and Violet really so unique?

Rose stole a glance at Jake. He observed the scene with the same mild curiosity he bestowed on everything. He spotted Rose watching him and his eyes twinkled. Would he feel the same grateful joy and overflowing love for her when their turn came? Then again, none of them had the Sheriff waiting to haul him away, either. Maybe he couldn't appreciate the moment with that hanging over his head.

The minister instructed Chuck to kiss the bride. Chuck looked back at Violet and burst out laughing. Then he stepped closer to her, struggling mightily to keep smiling through his tears. Every time he laughed, it came out as a sob.

He lifted Violet's veil, and Rose heard her sobbing and laughing along with Chuck. Chuck placed both hands on Violet's shoulders, bent toward her, and pecked her tenderly once on the lips. He didn't try to make it any more than that.

Then he took both of Violet's hands in his. Without looking at the minister, he led Violet to the back of the room, out of view.

The minister looked around for his next victim. "Who's next?"

Chapter 27

Mick stepped forward, and Iris joined him. Mick didn't wait for any invitation. He reached out and took Iris's hand and squeezed it tight. His presence calmed Iris, and her crying faded to nothing. The minister began his service again.

When Mick said "I do," to the vows, his voice boomed out through the room. Rather than the rapture Rose saw on Chuck's face, Mick's expression looked more like a frown. He set his jaw and clenched his teeth. Then Rose realized he was determined not to cry through his own wedding.

Rose couldn't see Iris's face, but she recognized the sound when she said, "I do." Rose knew her sister well enough to know the feeling behind that voice. It was a voice of laughter, of song, of exultant triumph.

In spite of all Iris's accusations about who killed Cornell, Rose loved Iris now. One look at Mick and Iris's hands, clenched together so tightly their knuckles shone white, proved they belonged together. They would hold onto each other, supporting and maintaining each other through every storm.

Iris transformed herself over the last three days. She used to be a dusty, callused, chaps-wearing cattle puncher who liked nothing better than to ride the range every day. Now she was a delicate, lovely, bewitching bride who carried this man's heart in the palm of her hand. That transformation happened when Iris met Mick McAllister. He made her what she was, and what she wanted to be.

The minister told Mick to kiss the bride. Mick glanced at him, just to make sure he hadn't heard wrong. Then he moved closer to Iris and lifted her veil.

When he saw her face, his resolve melted, and his mouth twisted up into a mask of emotion. His lips quivered, and his eyes overflowed the tears he held back during the ceremony. Iris's shoulders jerked once in laughter, and then she burst into tears, too.

Mick squeezed Iris's hand tighter than ever. He laid his other hand on her cheek and kissed her, but his lips wouldn't behave. As soon as they touched Iris's lips, they jerked away from her, and he broke down in wracking sobs. He threw both arms around Iris and wept on her shoulder.

Iris held him up with her slender arms around his ribs, patting him on the back between her own sobs. At last, she pushed him up and off of her, took him by the hand, and led him to the back of the room where Chuck and Violet waited for them.

And there they were, Jake and Rose, alone, staring at each other across the room.

The minister waited for them to move up, but neither moved a muscle.

Jake's eyes bored into Rose's brain, obliterating all awareness of everything else. Nothing remained in the world except him. She didn't know if she could move with him looking at her like that. A rabbit caught by the mesmerizing gaze of a wolf must feel this way. Her every fiber screamed for her to break that iron stare, but she couldn't move.

The minister affected to cough nervously to get their attention. Jake's eyes pierced her across the gulf. He tilted his head slightly to one side as if shrugging off the tension of the moment. Then he stood up from his chair.

With a sweeping motion, he moved the chair forward. Using the back of the chair like an improvised crutch, he hopped into the space left vacant by the other two couples.

Still she couldn't move. Only when he held out his hand to her did she find herself freed from her trance. She reached out her hand and grasped the life line he threw to her. He rescued her from drowning in the abyss and pulled her to the safety of the place in front of the minister.

As soon as they got into position, the minister examined the couple for a moment. "Aren't you going to take your hat off, young man?" he asked Jake.

Jake chuckled. "I suppose I could."

The minister scowled at him, and Jake lifted his hat off his head.

The other couples probably couldn't see well enough from the back of the room, but Rose saw the thick black thatch of his hair combed back from his forehead and down behind his ears.

He took the hat off with his left hand and set it on one of the side tables at his elbow, right next to one of the vases of daisies. Sheriff Maitland moved out of his place in the corner and stepped up toward Jake, staring hard at him. His eyes flashed, and he pressed his lips together.

"Is everything all right, Sheriff?" the minister asked.

The Sheriff glanced at the minister. Then he gave Jake one last hard stare and moved back. He nodded to the minister. "Carry on."

Rose didn't hear much of what the minister said. Something extraordinary was happening to her. She was changing again.

Just when she thought she was finished changing into a completely different person, now she experienced another transformation. Her mind seemed the same, but her body shifted and morphed into something completely alien to her.

She was becoming Mrs. Jacob Hamilton. Did she really want to become that? Just a few nights ago, her sisters asked her if she really wanted to go through with this wedding, and she insisted that she did. Only now did she really understand. Was this wise? Could a person undergo such a massive upheaval, such a fundamental alteration to their identity, and survive it? Would she fall apart into her component pieces?

Violet and Iris couldn't have gone through a similar experience when they said their vows. They were too happy, and they married men who acted as bedrock for their identities.

She stood alone with this feeling. Jake certainly didn't feel any uncertainty about getting married. He just asked her, not two hours ago, if she was his, and she said *Always*. Was she still his now?

Rose shuddered. Then she heard the minister addressing her. "Rose?"

"What?" she answered.

"Rose?" he repeated. "Did you hear me?"

"Hear what?" Rose reached up to brush something out of her face, but found her way blocked by her veil. Then she realized the thing she wanted to brush away *was* the veil, and she lowered her hand to her bouquet again.

"I read you your vows," the minister told her. "We'll start again. Don't drift off, because it's important you know what you're agreeing to. Do you, Rose, take this man Jacob, as your lawfully wedded husband, to love, honor, and obey him, forsaking all others, for better or for worse, in sickness and in health, 'til death do you part?"

"I do," she replied.

The minister stared at her. "Are you sure?"

"Of course, I'm sure," Rose shot back. "You just heard me say I do, didn't you?"

"Okay," the minister replied. "I just wanted to be sure.

You didn't hear me the first time, so I just thought I'd check. If you're sure, that's all that matters."

"Why wouldn't I be sure?" Rose snapped.

"Very well," the minister answered.

He prattled on about something or other, and then he told Jake, "You may kiss the bride."

What an anti-climax! They'd already kissed a dozen times in stolen moments like this morning in the Bird House and this afternoon in the canyon. And here they were, supposed to kiss in front of her sisters and their new husbands and Sheriff Tom Maitland, as if they would put their passion for each other on public display!

Chapter 28

Jake acted so self-assured. But when he stood before her, his lips twitching one way and another under his moustache in their approach to her mouth, she saw the hesitation in his eyes. That was never there before.

Just before he kissed her, he glanced toward the back of the room, toward the Sheriff.

He kissed her, a casual, platonic, Aunt Polly sort of kiss that meant nothing. Then he stepped back and chuckled. Rose's mind spun in confusion. Should she be horrified or relieved that it was over? And now there was nothing stopping the Sheriff from dragging him away. But there was no backing out now. The deed was done. They were married.

She felt him take her hand, and they turned away from the minister toward the others. Rose scanned their faces and burst into tears all over again.

Her sisters surrounded her, comforting her, misunderstanding her tears for tears of joy. They embraced her and wept along with her, while their men slapped each other on the back and shook each other's hands.

Rose's sisters let her go just enough for her to get a look at Jake. He laughed and joked with the others, but when he caught her eye, some question lurked there below the surface. He didn't offer the salvation from uncertainty she thought he would.

She thought all she had to do was marry him, and everything else would be okay. Now they were married, for better or for worse, and everything would not be okay—not by a long way

How much did she really know about him? Nothing. Wasn't that the whole point of marrying a mail-order husband? You never knew what you were going to get. Had she grossly misjudged not only him, but this whole marriage proposition, too? What if it didn't do what she wanted it to do? What if it didn't offer her the shelter and protection she hoped it would? Where would she be then?

If that happened, she'd be utterly lost. She'd be as good as dead.

But no one seemed to notice any change except her. If anything, marriage somehow redeemed Jake in the eyes of his new in-laws. They managed to forget their suspicions of him and welcomed him into the fold of the newly married.

Where had the minister gone? He'd vanished somewhere, along with the Sheriff. May he vanish forever into the shadows and never bother her or her family again! But that wouldn't happen. She could only rest for a few moments until he came back, asking questions and seeing things she'd just as soon he didn't see.

What torment Violet must have gone through before he pried the truth out of her about beating up Cornell! At least she had that out in the open. No wonder she could enjoy her wedding, even with the Sheriff poking around. He already knew the worst there was to know about her.

Rose shuddered and let her sisters comfort her. They probably would have stood there, leaking at the eyelids, all day long if good, staunch Violet hadn't intervened. "Let's get out of this parlor!" she blurted out. "Let's get over to the dining room, and we can all sit down and have something to eat. We can relax there, or we can go sit in the front sitting room."

With a gaggle of conversation, the three couples repaired to the dining room. But no one seemed all that interested in food, except the minister, who materialized from his hiding place just in time to eat.

Jake leaned on Rose's arm and hopped from one room to the other. As they entered the dining room, Rita set a platter of steaming roast beef on one of the side tables and went out to the kitchen for more. The three couples wandered around in a daze, but none of them sat down.

"I wonder if the Sheriff wants to eat something before he heads back to Butte," Violet murmured.

"Where is he?" Iris whispered back. "I didn't see where he went."

"Maybe he went to get his horse out," Mick suggested.

"I don't think he'll wait long enough to eat," Chuck remarked.

They didn't have long to wait, however. The Sheriff strutted into the room before the words finished coming out of his mouth.

"Come on, Hamilton," he announced. "Time to go."

Chapter 29

"Wait!" Rose cried. "You can't go yet."

The Sheriff scowled at her. "Why not? I told you I'd wait long enough for you two to get married. That's done. Now it's time to leave."

Violet stepped in. "Would you like to eat something before you leave, Sheriff? There's plenty here. We don't want the food going to waste."

"No, I don't want to eat anything," Sheriff Maitland thundered. "I want to take this man back to Butte to stand trial for Cornell Pollard's death. That's what I came here for, and that's what I'm going to do. Now, come on!"

Even as he said these words, a thought crossed his mind, and he came up close to Jake's face, peering at him hard in the brighter light of the dining room.

"Is anything wrong, Sheriff?" Chuck asked.

"What is....." He pointed toward Jake's head, "what is that?"

Everyone in the room craned their necks to see what the Sheriff was pointing at.

"What are you looking at?" Iris asked.

"Look," Sheriff Maitland barked. "Look hard. You can't see it very well because his hair is black. But it's there."

"What is?" Chuck asked.

"Look!" the Sheriff shouted. The newlyweds surrounded Jake and stared at his head as hard as the Sheriff did until they all saw a crust of black just inside his hairline above his left ear. "Now do you see it?"

"What is it?" Iris asked.

"Ask him that," Sheriff Maitland screamed. "Tell us, Hamilton. What is it?"

"I hurt myself," Jake murmured.

Violet's head swung around and she gasped, staring at Rose.

"*How* did you hurt yourself?" the sheriff demanded.

"I fell over," Jake replied.

"*How* did you fall over?" Sheriff Maitland yelled.

Jake lowered his eyes to the floor. "Does it really matter?"

"Of course it matters!" the sheriff boomed. "You killed him, didn't you? You killed Cornell Pollard."

"Sheriff!" Violet cried. "You can't mean it!"

"I do mean it," the sheriff shot back. "I wasn't completely certain before, but I am now. Do you know how he got that injury on his head, and the other one on his arm? Cornell hit him with the poker from the fireplace in the library. I noticed a stain of dried blood on the hook of the poker when I examined the room, but I didn't think anything about it at the time. Now I know where it came from."

The other newlyweds gasped in shock at the revelation. Rose quailed, and her stomach wrenched into a ball of knots.

Violet turned to her. "Rose, did you…?" She stopped.

"Sheriff," Rose began, "you can't do this! You don't understand."

"Don't try to defend him now, Rose," Mick growled. "He's a murderer."

Rose choked on her sobs. "He is not a murderer. He didn't kill Cornell."

Mick rounded on her with his teeth bared. "You're delusional, if you think he's innocent. All the evidence points to him. You just love him too much to admit it. He's a snake in the grass, and he somehow managed to rope you into believing he's innocent so you'll tell everyone so at every opportunity. Anybody can see that."

Rose shook her head, and tears flew away from her face. "It isn't true! You're wrong."

"You haven't given anybody any reason to think otherwise," he pointed out. "And neither has Jake. You've both gone out of your way to confirm your guilt in everyone's minds. You've been more concerned about moving into the Bird House than with proving your innocence."

"That's not true!" Rose wailed.

Mick clenched his jaw and turned away. Violet stepped up again. "She's distraught over Jake leaving. Just let her alone, and she'll come around."

"I will not come around!" Rose shrieked. "I will not see sense, or snap out of it, or any other words you want to use to say that I will think Jake is guilty because he isn't. Now stop saying that!"

She stared wildly from one face to another, but they all closed to her with their mouths clamped shut and their eyes narrowed.

In the end, Iris came toward her. "Listen, Rose. You have to admit to yourself that the evidence is overwhelming. He's the only one who could have killed Cornell. Admit it. He's going to Butte to face justice, and that's the best place for him."

"I'll tell you what," Sheriff Maitland put in. "I'll show you the evidence for yourself. I'll show you the inside of his gun, where it left the marks on the bullets that killed Cornell. Will that convince you?"

Rose shook her head, distracted with grief and fear, but Sheriff Maitland ignored her. "Give me your side arms," he said to Jake.

Jake pulled out one of his pistols. He flipped it around and passed it, butt first, to the Sheriff. Sheriff Maitland pulled back the hammer and opened the tumbler. He examined the interior of the firing chamber. Then he smelled the gun before handing it back to Jake. "And the other one?"

Jake handed over his other pistol and the Sheriff gave it the same inspection. But this time, when he looked down into the firing chamber, his eyes lit up. "Ah-ha! Right here!"

He held the gun open for all to see. "You see those little spikes of metal sticking out of the wall there? They left the marks on the bullet I took from Cornell. That proves it." He held the gun aloft. "This is the murder weapon."

His performance didn't ruffle Jake in the slightest. "And I suppose you kept the bullet to match to the gun."

"You would think of something like that, wouldn't you?" Sheriff Maitland shot back. "As a matter of fact, I did keep the bullet, and the district attorney can present that evidence at the trial. So you might as well tell us all how it happened. Tell us how Cornell Pollard died."

Jake cocked his head on one side. "I really don't know how he died."

The Sheriff snorted. "What? Are you really going to stand there and tell me and all the rest of these people that this gun didn't kill him? Are you going to tell us you were nowhere near the library at the time of his death? You can't expect us to believe that."

"I didn't say the gun didn't kill him," Jake replied. "And I didn't say I wasn't in the library. But I didn't kill him."

"Then how did he die?" Sheriff Maitland demanded again. "Tell us."

"I really don't know," Jake insisted. "I would tell you if I could."

"Stop!" Rose wailed. "Please stop!"

She covered her ears with her both hands, and her sleeves fell back around her elbows.

Chapter 30

"Rose!" Violet gasped. "Rose, your arm!"

Sheriff Maitland stared at Rose's arm. "Miss?" he gasped. "How did you get that mark on your arm?"

Rose sank into a chair, covered her face with her hands, and sobbed. "You don't understand. Jake didn't kill Cornell. You can't take him in. He's innocent."

"Young lady," Sheriff Maitland rumbled. "If you have something to tell me, now is the time to do it."

Jake hopped over to her. "Say it, Rose. Say it now."

Rose lifted her face to him. Tears stained her cheeks. She opened her mouth, but faltered when she saw her sisters staring at her with their jaws hanging open. "I can't!"

"Rose," Jake continued, "if you don't say it now, I'm going to be hauled off to jail as a murderer. We'll probably never see each other again. You have to say it now."

Rose covered her face again, the sobs ripping out of her chest in great wrenching bursts.

"I killed Cornell!" she blurted out. "I killed him!"

"You!" Violet gasped. "Not you!"

Jake held up his hand. "Don't accuse her until you hear the whole story. She kept silent all this time because she didn't

131

want you and Iris to know. She thought you wouldn't be able to forgive her for killing him."

"But how....?" Iris asked.

Jake faced the company. "After we got back from Butte and had supper, Chuck and Violet went out for a walk. I guess Mick and Iris went off to the barn together. Rose and I went out the back door. We sat on that bench by the back shed, just sitting and watching the moonlight over the land. We didn't say much. We just sat there, holding hands."

"Did you hear the scuffle between Violet and Cornell?" the Sheriff asked.

"We heard something," Jake admitted, "because Rose came back inside. After a while, I heard another noise. I don't know what it was, but I came in to find out if Rose was okay and to check and see if she was coming back out to me or if I should head back to the Fort House. I found her in the front hall."

"Was Cornell still there?" Violet asked.

Jake nodded. "Rose and Cornell were talking about something. They were speaking in quiet voices, so I couldn't understand what they were saying. I came into the hall, and I walked right up to them. I asked Rose if everything was okay. She didn't answer me."

"Did Cornell say anything?" Iris asked.

"Not right away," Jake replied. "So I tried to introduce myself. I stuck out my hand and said, 'I'm Jake Hamilton, pleased to make your acquaintance, you must be Cornell Pollard, I've heard a lot about you'—all the usual stuff."

"What was his reaction?" Chuck asked.

"He didn't react at all," Jake told him. "He turned around and walked away into the library. Rose and I followed him in there, and Rose started talking to him. She said she was marrying me, and the least he could do was behave civilly toward us."

"What happened then?" Sheriff Maitland asked.

"He picked up the poker and started smashing the place up," Jake recalled. "He moved so fast that he caught me off guard. I didn't see the poker coming the first time, and he hooked me in the side of the arm. He swung it around a couple of times, just slashing the air with it. But then he aimed and caught me on the side of the head. I fell over, and I don't know what happened after that."

Everyone turned on Rose, who sat crying into her hands.

"Rose?" the Sheriff asked. "What did you do when Cornell hit Jake in the head with the poker?"

She didn't answer.

"She's been out of her mind with worry that her sisters would find out," Jake told him.

"She didn't act very out of her mind with worry," Iris put in. "She acted like she didn't care at all that Cornell was dead."

"She had to act that way," Jake told her. "She had to cover it up to stop you finding out she killed him. She wouldn't even say the words to me. I only knew she did it because I was there. She wouldn't talk about it at all. She couldn't admit it even to herself."

"Rose," Sheriff Maitland told her, "I still need to hear from you exactly what happened. I can't release Jake until you tell me the whole story."

"I killed him," she wailed. "I said I killed him. Isn't that enough?"

"No, it isn't," the Sheriff pressed her. "I need to know what happened so I know that you killed him in defense of your own life and Jake's life. If you don't tell me that, I can't release Jake or you. Now tell me. Once you get it out in the open, you'll feel much better and you can put the whole thing behind you."

Rose sobbed into her hands a while longer. Finally, she collected herself enough to start talking. "I saw Jake fall down in front of the window. I thought he was dead, but Cornell wouldn't stop waving that poker around."

"Did he go after you with it?" Sheriff Maitland asked.

Rose shook her head. "He didn't pay any attention to me. He just kept going after Jake. I guess after his fight with Chuck and Violet, he had a vendetta against all three of the men. Jake was lying on the floor, not moving, and Cornell raised the poker over his head to smash him again. I dove on top of him and covered him with my body. I got my arm up just in time to block the poker from coming down on top of Jake again."

"He must have hit you pretty hard, to make that mark," Iris pointed out.

"I thought my arm was broken," Rose replied, "and he just picked up the poker and was going to hit us again. He would have kept hitting us again and again until he beat us to death. I'm convinced of it."

"So what did you do?" Sheriff Maitland asked.

"I didn't really think about it," Rose told him. "I never made the decision to do anything. Something just took over my body, and the next minute, I found Jake's pistol in my hand and I shot at Cornell. I didn't even really understand what happened until Cornell fell over."

"How did you get out of the library in time for me to find the body?" Violet asked.

"After Cornell fell over," Rose replied. "I felt Jake moving underneath me and I realized he was still alive. I pulled him to his feet and pulled him out of the house. As soon as we got out the back door, the cool air sort of revived him. I snuck back in through the back door and met Iris on the stairs. Jake went around through the kitchen door and met up with Mick. We all came to the library together and found you standing over Cornell's body."

"But we didn't see any signs of struggle on you then," Iris pointed out. "We didn't see any blood on your clothes or on your face or head. How do you explain that?"

"You may recall," Jake replied, "that I was wearing a dark

suit, so you wouldn't have seen the blood on my arm. And my hair is black, and it was dark in the library. I kept the blood on my head concealed in my hair and under my hat, and by keeping that side of my head turned away from you. Then I made myself scarce."

Chapter 31

"Oh, darling!" Violet threw herself on her knees in front of Rose. "Why didn't you tell me before? You know I never would have accused you if I had known."

"I just couldn't face you," Rose sobbed. "I couldn't say the words out loud, 'I killed Cornell, Violet.' I couldn't. I just couldn't."

"Rose told me not to tell anyone," Jake told the Sheriff. "I advised her to tell the truth from the start, but she insisted we keep quiet. She didn't want anyone to know she killed Cornell, even though she did it in self-defense."

The Sheriff scowled at him. Then he hitched his thumbs into his belt and stood back. "I don't like it at all. I ought to charge both of you for withholding vital evidence. But under the circumstances, I'll let it drop."

"So you believe Rose's story?" Violet asked. "She never hurt a fly in her life before. If she shot and killed Cornell, you can be certain she did it under the most dire circumstances."

Sheriff Maitland gazed down at Rose. "I believe that. From what Violet told us about her confrontation with him, I think we can all assume that Cornell lost control of himself, probably in response to you ladies marrying against his wishes. He lost control, and he turned violent, first with Mr. Ahern, then with Violet, and finally, with you and Mr. Hamilton. I also believe what you said when you told me he wouldn't stop until he beat you to death. The only way to stop him killing you and Mr. Hamilton was for you to kill him first."

Rose looked up at him and sniffed. "You won't take Jake away, will you? Not now that you know the truth?"

"No," Sheriff Maitland replied. "I'm releasing him without charge. But you could have avoided this whole misunderstanding by telling me the truth from the beginning. You could have saved us all a lot of trouble."

Rose hung her head. "I'm sorry about that. I just didn't want anyone to know. I didn't want my sisters to think I was a killer."

"You're not a killer," Sheriff Maitland told her. "Killing someone in self-defense doesn't make you a killer. If anyone's a killer, it's Cornell."

Violet sighed. "Now that we've got that cleared up, Sheriff, are you sure you won't stay and enjoy our wedding feast with us. We have a cake and a lot of good food to eat yet."

"Thank you, Miss," he replied, "but I won't stay. I have a long way to go before I get back to Butte, and I'll have some explaining to do when I get there. I still have to report to the county prosecutor on the outcome of my investigation, and the local paper ran a story on Cornell's death. They'll want to know the upshot of the investigation, too. I'm sure the minister will help you dispose of the food."

Violet laughed. "I'm sure he will. I just don't want you to leave without knowing you're welcome, and that none of us bears you any ill will for your part in this."

Sheriff Maitland tipped his hat. "I appreciate that. I've done my best to bring Cornell's killer to justice. Now I realize that I have by leaving these two love birds here to start their new life together." He looked back down at Rose. "It seems to me, Miss, that you'll have all you can handle just living with Cornell's death on your conscience. Take my word for it and don't be too hard on yourself. It could take a while before you put this situation behind you and realize that you didn't do anything wrong."

Rose bowed her head and her tears fell into her lap. She watched the droplets spread through the woven fabric of her wedding dress. "Thank you."

The Sheriff tipped his hat again and strode out of the house. He untied his horse from the corner of the porch and mounted to his saddle.

"You folks have a good evening," he called. "Don't eat too much."

He wheeled his horse around and trotted off into the west where the setting sun dipped behind the mountains.

The three couples watched him from the front door.

"There he goes," Iris remarked.

"I wonder if we'll see him again soon," Chuck added.

"I hope not," Mick replied.

He and Iris went back inside to the dining room. Chuck and Violet joined them, and they sat down at the table with the minister for the meal.

Rose hung around the doorway, staring over the range to the hazy purple mountains beyond. Blessed silence enveloped the ranch.

"Hey." Jake's voice made her start, and she found him standing next to her. "We're married now." He took her hand. "You're not having second thoughts, are you?"

"Second thoughts?" she asked.

"About marrying me," he explained.

She shook her head. "No. I was just thinking. After the ceremony, I wondered why marrying you didn't solve anything or make me feel as safe and protected as I thought it should. Now I know why."

Jake cocked his head. "Why?"

"I was scared," she told him. "I was scared all the time that someone would find out. Marrying you didn't solve that, and it didn't take my fear away. That's why marrying you didn't make me feel safe and protected."

"So how do you feel now?" he asked.

A brilliant smile broke across her face. "Light." She raised her arms. "Free. I feel like I could rise up off the ground and float away. It wasn't marrying you that made me feel safe and happy. It was everybody finding out my secret. I don't have to worry anymore about them finding out, because they already know, and they forgive me for it."

"They don't forgive you," Jake corrected her. "There's nothing to forgive. You didn't do anything wrong."

Rose gazed toward the sunset. "He's right. It's going to take a long time before I'm ready to believe that. I took a gun and shot a man in the head. I have to carry that with me for the rest of my life."

"That just goes to show you're a good person," Jake pointed out. "If anyone here had the right to kill him, it's you. After what he did, killing him was the right thing to do. You and I both have the marks to prove it."

"I know," Rose replied. "I know that in my head, but my heart still doesn't want to believe I really did it."

Jake studied her face. "You say you feel light and free, but you look like you're ready to fall over. You look exhausted."

"How can I be exhausted?" she asked. "I haven't really done much of anything other than ride up into the canyon and walk back again."

"I mean you look emotionally exhausted," Jake told her. "You look like you're about to fall apart."

She smiled, but a wave of oppressive weariness overwhelmed her. "You're right. Holding back my feelings really took its toll on me."

Jake hopped over to her and wrapped his arms around her shoulders. Her head fell onto his shoulder and he hugged her to his chest. "Let's go sit down. You can have something to eat, and then we'll go up to the Bird House and go to bed. How does that sound?"

"It sounds wonderful," she replied. "What about the minister?"

"I think he's going back to Butte, too," Jake told her, "just as soon as he's eaten."

"Did Violet arrange that?" Rose asked.

Jake chuckled. "I don't think so. I think he's planning to enjoy one last meal and then skedaddle." Jake kissed her on the forehead. "Come on. You're tired, and my leg hurts, and Violet won't let us go until we've eaten our share of the food."

Chapter 32

Evening faded away to night, and the three couples pushed their stuffed bellies away from the dining room table.

"I suppose you'll all be going home to your own houses now." Violet touched her handkerchief to the corner of her eyes.

"And don't forget," Iris reminded her, "you and Chuck are going home to your own room in your own house. You'll have the place to yourselves."

Violet laughed and wiped away her tears. "You won't believe this, but I had forgotten. Can you believe it? I was so concerned about losing you two that I forgot all about my own wedding night!" She sobbed, and Chuck took her hand.

Mick patted his stomach. "I couldn't eat another thing. I think I'll head up to bed."

Iris smiled at him. "Do you mind if I join you?"

"I was hoping you would," he replied.

"We'll head home, too," Jake announced. "Rose is worn out, and I've got to put my leg up. It aches somethin' awful."

"Do you need any help tending it?" Violet offered.

"Thank you," Jake replied, "but I'll get Rose to tend it for me."

"Oh!" Violet exclaimed. "Of course! I'm so sorry."

"You'll have to get used to leaving people alone, Violet," Iris told her. "I think a lot of things are going to change around here from now on."

"And all for the better," Rose added.

"I'll miss you all," Violet sobbed.

Rose got up and went to her. "We aren't going anywhere. We'll see you in the morning, the same as always. We're right nearby, and we all agreed that we'll be in each other's lives for a long time to come."

Violet threw her arms around Rose. "Oh, Rose! Can you ever forgive us for tormenting you these last few days? We never should have let our petty suspicions get in the way of family."

"I should have trusted you," Rose replied. "I should have trusted you enough to tell you the truth. It's me who should be asking you to forgive me."

Iris rose from her seat. "No, it's me who should be asking your forgiveness, Rose. I never should have accused you. I should have stood by you just as firmly as Violet did."

"You had every reason to accuse me," Rose maintained. "You had every right to demand an explanation, and I should have given you one."

Mick stood up and walked over to Jake's chair. He put out his hand, "Jake Hamilton, let me shake your hand. You're not the man I thought you were. You're ten times the man I thought you were, and I'm sorry I misjudged you. I hope you can see clear to putting this misunderstanding behind us, and I hope you will forgive me for thinking you murdered Cornell. I should have minded my own business until all the evidence was on the table instead of runnin' off half-cocked."

Jake pushed himself up from his chair with his hands propped on the table. Then he shook Mick's hand. "Let's all put this nightmare behind us. When we first came home from Butte, we had a good idea of how to move forward and run this ranch together. Cornell dying threw a wrench in those plans. Now we can go ahead and build the life we all dreamed of. We can make Rocking Horse Ranch the thriving concern we all want it to be. Let's pledge ourselves to that now."

Chuck and Violet came to them, and the six newlyweds shook hands and embraced and reaffirmed their commitment to their shared future as a family.

After all the promises and all the tears of joy and relief, Mick and Iris made their way to the front door to take their leave. The three sisters threw themselves into each other's arms all over again and wept at Iris's departure.

"Don't worry," she told them. "I'm sure I'll be down first thing in the morning to get some food for breakfast. I'm sure these men didn't leave a crumb in the house for us."

Chuck and Mick grinned at each other. "Of course we didn't."

Mick took Iris by the hand, and they strolled away toward the Fort House, waving over their shoulders and calling out, "Good-bye!"

Violet and Rose watched them go with tears streaming down their cheeks until Chuck stepped up and closed the door in their faces, preventing them from seeing Mick and Iris all the way to the Fort House door.

They laughed at him and cried some more, and then Jake took Rose by the hand and led her to the back door of the house.

Violet and Rose embraced, and cried more pitifully than ever at this last farewell. "Now promise me you'll come down first thing in the morning, too. I want to see both you and Iris for breakfast."

"I won't promise that," Rose replied. "I might want to spend just a little time alone with Jake tomorrow. But I'll be down. You don't have to worry about that. I'm not leaving. I'm just a few steps away. After this honeymoon is over, you'll be able to come up and see me whenever you want."

"How long is the honeymoon likely to take?" Violet asked.

Rose laughed. "How you do talk! What about you? You're not going to want me and Iris barging in on you and Chuck at odd times. You might want to see us again, but you won't want your house to turn into a jolly convention center, you know."

Violet laughed and dabbed her tears away.

Then Jake took Rose's hand again and refused to let her be drawn back in. Step by step, he pulled her up the path, waving good-bye to Chuck and Violet.

Rose glanced over her shoulder and waved and sobbed, until Chuck closed that door, too. All of a sudden, Rose found herself on the outside of the Main House, closed off from her past life and consigned, for good, to the future.

Jake led her up the path and behind the hedge, but he stopped in the garden. "Here we are."

"Here we are," she agreed.

He took her in his arms. "Welcome home."

The End

Thank you for reading and supporting my book and I hope you enjoyed it.

Please will you do me a favor and review "Rose's Mail Order Husband" so I'll know whether you liked it or not, it would be very much appreciated, thank you.

Connect With Kate

Visit my website at www.katewhitsby.com to sign up to my newsletter so that you will be notified as to when my new releases are available.

Other Books by Kate Whitsby

Alma's Mail Order Husband (Texas Brides: Book 1)
Mail Order Marion (Chapman Mail Order Brides: Book 1)
Christmas Mail Order Bride
Mail Order Josephine
Mail Order Bride Romance Box Set
Western Mail Order Brides Box Set

About Kate Whitsby

Kate Whitsby is a historical romance author who has found a love for writing western mail order bride romance. Kate writes from her home in Virginia and loves spending time with her two children when she's not busy writing.

Copyright

© 2014 by Kate Whitsby

All Rights Reserved. No part of this publication may be copied, reproduced in any format, by any means, electronic or otherwise, without prior consent from the copyright owner and publisher of this book.

This is a work of fiction. All characters, names, places and events are the product of the author's imagination or used fictitiously.

Manufactured by Amazon.ca
Bolton, ON